Floodwood

Pete Kennedy

HIGHPOINT
LIT

This edition published by Highpoint Lit, an imprint of Highpoint Executive Publishing.
For information, write to info@highpointpubs.com.

First Edition
ISBN: 978-1-7344497-9-2

Kennedy, Pete
Floodwood

Summary: "There's something rotten at New York's prestigious Strabo Society, and a werewolf is on the loose in sedate Westchester County. Improbably assisted by an intrepid female professor-turned-secret-agent named Artemis Fletcher, the werewolf's mission is anything but expected, spanning the globe from the Adirondacks to the Himalayas and ancient temples of Japan. This unforgettable mystery novel combines classical and folk mythology, esoteric tropes and a touch of horror that recalls Edgar Allen Poe and Mary Shelley." – Provided by publisher.

ISBN: 978-1-7344497-9-2 (paperback)

Library of Congress Control Number: 2021909804

Cover illustration by Jennifer Lenox, Vermont artist
Cover concept by Maura Kennedy
Interior design by Sarah M. Clarehart

10 9 8 7 6 5 4 3 2 1

CONTENTS

ACKNOWLEDGMENTS

Thanks to Maura Kennedy, Michael Roney, and Lori Paximadis, who shepherded the story along and made this a better book. Thanks also to Sarah Clarehart for the creative interior design, Jen Lenox for the great painting, with special thanks to John and Suzy Allman, who first introduced me to Floodwood Pond.

PART ONE

The Pond

We know what we are, but not what we are to be.

—Pythagoras

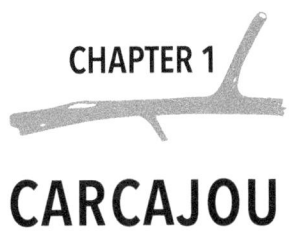

CHAPTER 1

CARCAJOU

October 1920, Adirondack State Park

A twig snapped.

Cardonas woke suddenly. There was a rustling sound behind the tent. He lit a match and squinted at his pocket watch. It was 4 a.m. He lay in his sleeping bag, frozen in fear. High in the white pine, an owl shrieked. Another twig snapped, this time directly in front of his tent. Cardonas crawled forward, too terrified to lie still. Maybe he could make a dash to the canoe, push off, and be safe in open water. He untied the twine and opened the flaps.

He was staring directly into a pair of blazing yellow eyes.

CHAPTER 2

THE ASSIGNMENT

One week earlier, Strabo Society headquarters, New York City

Over lunch at the club, Duncan Sinclair spelled out the mission for Cardonas. Two years had passed since fire swept through the heart of the Adirondacks. Hillsides lay exposed that had hidden their secrets for centuries. There was a rush to uncover what might be revealed before fast-growing maples and conifers reclaimed the forest. There were places, reachable only by canoe, where priceless antiquities lay waiting to be found and spirited out to private clubs and lodges in the city. Duncan Sinclair had become fixated on adding a Neolithic stone weapon to the Strabo Society's collection.

There was a controversy in the geographers' community over whether the Iroquois had established villages in the region or had just traveled in and out on hunting expeditions. Given the importance of the beaver pelt trade in New York history, the society that added a piece to the puzzle would top the list for lucrative grants, and the scientist who brought a crucial artifact back from the field would be in line for the Strabo Medal.

Sinclair gave Cardonas a simple formula. Pot shards and cooking utensils would equal longhouse towns. Arrowheads and spearheads would indicate hunting grounds. He wrote out the mission details on Society letterhead, dated October 20, 1920.

Mission: Search for Iroquois stone artifacts.
Location: Adirondack State Park.
Eyes only: No permits. Artifacts carried out in camping gear.
Party: Anthony Cardonas (leader) Alistair Wulver (assistant).

Cardonas read the memo and scowled.

"Wulver? You're saddling me with that greenhorn and his mystic mumbo-jumbo? You expect me to be subjected to three days in a canoe listening to his endless tales of everything from reincarnation to the significance of zombie ritual? He's not a scientist, Duncan, and I don't for the life of me understand why you even entertain the idea of bringing him into the society."

"Anthony, listen to me. It's all about Lethe Van Leer, his guardian out there in Westchester. You know he's a club founder and a major donor. I can't cross him without risking a dent in the Society's endowment."

"Understood. I will grit my teeth and try to tolerate the neophyte, Duncan. You know full well that I'm determined to come back with a major artifact, and when I do, I expect you to personally nominate me for the Strabo Medal. Furthermore, if I have to put up with that twit Wulver, I'm not sharing the glory with anyone."

"I didn't say anything about sharing, Anthony. Besides…"

Sinclair took a sip from his single-malt Scotch.

"Who knows what might happen up in the St. Regis wilderness at this deserted time of year?"

The two men rose and shook hands.

CHAPTER 3

THE JOURNEY

The star-crossed explorers mustered on Tuesday, October 26, at Gate 13, Penn Station. They shook hands formally, without warmth, and boarded the 9 p.m. New York Central Ontarian, a sleeper train heading straight north up the Hudson. The men conversed stiffly over cocktails as the train trundled past the palisades on the opposite bank. Cardonas, in a pinstriped Brooks Brothers suit with his dark hair slicked back and parted in the middle, Ivy League style, was the picture of Manhattan sophistication. He stroked his waxed mustache absently and fixed his gaze out the train window when Wulver spoke, putting on a show of disdain for the younger man's notions. Wulver's unruly blond hair fell across his collar, and he lounged in casual twill chinos on the polished oak bench, like a youthful Greek philosopher at the School of Athens. As the train crossed to the west riverside at Albany to continue north, the mismatched travelers retired to their Pullman coach stateroom. Wulver, younger and more spry, took the upper bunk. As the train wended its way past

Lake George, the men conversed about scientific matters, and the conversation soon turned to disagreement.

Cardonas had always considered Lethe Van Leer an eccentric. As an empiricist, he had no time for what he considered frivolous, unprovable speculation. A few minutes of conversation with his bunkmate confirmed his suspicion that the young man had been thoroughly indoctrinated by Van Leer in his brand of hazy mysticism. When he returned to the city, he would give Sinclair a piece of his mind. He might have simply given the young man the silent treatment, but that was not Cardonas's way. Always imperious, he seized any opportunity to belittle those he thought inferior, which was basically anyone not brandishing an open checkbook.

"Wulver, listen to me. If you actually aspire to membership in the Strabo Society, I beg you to toss away those ancient books to which you seem compelled to refer. That's superstition, not science. You don't reach a lost continent by reading Plato's account of Atlantis. You wrap yourself in sealskin like Amundsen did, and go there! There was a man of vision. Ice and snow, that was his vision, not some mumbo-jumbo written by a reclining wine drinker in ancient Greece."

"What if Plato was right about Atlantis?"

"Fine! Then go there, and bring something back to the club. A mermaid, perhaps. Maybe she could tell us all about the flood, and you could bag the Strabo Medal."

Cardonas's patronizing line of verbal abuse was relentless. Wulver rolled over in his upper bunk and switched off the overhead light. At dawn they would disembark at Saranac Lake Village, in the heart of the Adirondacks.

CHAPTER 4

THE OUTPOST

Cardonas tipped the porter a nickel as their bags were offloaded onto the platform. Each man had two Army surplus duffels. One would hold their city clothes and toiletries, to be left at the hotel while they were in the bush, and the other held a few camping essentials: a canteen, mess kit, khaki shirt and trousers, a compass, and a basic first aid kit. Those would go with them into the field. The rest of the necessaries, including a tent and canoe, would be obtained from Jacques Dubois, an outfitter on the north shore of Floodwood Pond, deep in the St. Regis wilderness.

The men boarded another train, this time a narrow-gauge electric rail line that ran exclusively to the St. Regis Hotel. The hotel, which had started out as a primitive hunting cabin decades earlier, was universally known as Paul Smith's Hotel. Smith's properties had grown from the cabin to a full-scale luxury hotel with its own rail line, both powered by his electric generating plant which also served the "great camps," massive log cabins that formed a sort of Newport-like millionaires enclave on Spitfire Lake.

By late October, the great camps were boarded up. The blue-blooded residents and their servants were safely ensconced back in the city, in time for opera season. Cardonas knew it was the perfect chance to secure and safely smuggle out an artifact, the artifact that would elevate him to the upper echelon of the New York geographers' community. By this time next year, he wouldn't be sleeping in a pup tent.

Cardonas and Wulver checked in at the St. Regis front desk, leaving word that they would be camping in the lake wilderness for two nights, returning only to retrieve their city clothes and check out, room and tax to be charged to the Society. That squared away, they dressed for the field and met a hired car, another Paul Smith amenity, in front of the hotel. They loaded their camp duffels in a black Ford Model A, and the touring car rumbled south on highways 30 and 3 to the turnoff for the logging road that led west into the forest and Dubois's cabin. Ten bumpy miles of accordion road later, the Ford came to a stop at the outpost, the first building they had seen since they left the main road.

Dubois pulled the duffels out of the trunk and carried them, one on each arm, down to the waterside. Seeing that Wulver was younger, he stowed the rented pup tent, poles, and stakes in Alistair's duffel. He stuffed the packs under the wooden thwarts and nodded approvingly at his work. Then he motioned for his clients to follow him up the bank to his cabin. Dubois poured coffee from a tin pot hanging over an open fire, and the three men stood on the porch looking out across the pond, which was actually a sizable lake dotted with islands. Unlike Spitfire Lake, Floodwood had no great camps; in fact, it had no dwellings at all. The shoreline was a patchwork of new-growth conifers and still-burned areas. Cardonas decided to use the porch vantage point to sketch a map of visibly burned patches that might reveal native artifacts. Before doing so, though, he was compelled to establish alpha dominance in the little group. He addressed the outfitter.

"Jacques Dubois, eh? A regular Jack o' the Woods!"

Dubois looked out impassively over the lake. He didn't turn to face Cardonas. "An Anglo might translate it that way."

Cardonas began silently composing a follow-up insult, hoping to escalate the game, but Dubois spoke first.

"You *messieurs* are from New York City, yes? Let me tell you something about Floodwood. In the city, you have your police, you have your mayor, you have your governor Al Smith over all, no?"

"Of course, Dubois. That's called civilization."

"I want for you to be careful out there on the lake. You have left civilization behind. We have our own police, mayor, and governor here."

"Oh, really now? And who might they be?" Cardonas was warming up to a fresh argument.

"The black bear is our policeman. He takes orders from no one. When he is hungry, he eats. If he finds no food, he eats your food. The beaver is our mayor. He builds and maintains, and keeps watch over the shoreline. He decides where you can navigate a stream and where you must portage."

"And who, pray tell, is the governor?" Cardonas spoke as if teasing a small child.

Dubois tamped and then lit his calabash pipe.

"Carcajou." He said the word softly, almost under his breath.

"Pardon?" Cardonas used the French emphasis.

"Carcajou."

Cardonas snorted. "My dear fellow, I'm sure you must be referring to the wolverine, the nearest specimen of which is at least a hundred miles north of where we stand."

Wulver spoke, for the first time on the porch.

"The Latin name is *Gulo gulo,* the glutton. The fiercest animal in North America. They are also called the skunk bear, for the musk they secrete."

"All the more reason, my dear easily frightened boys, to be glad that we are far south of their territory," Cardonas adopted his trademark mocking tone.

Dubois took a puff on his calabash and spoke. "Carcajou will travel hundreds of miles to survey his domain."

He gestured at a birch-limb rack that held a dozen pelts—beaver, martin, mink—drying in the afternoon sun.

"Do you think that if Dubois can smuggle *castor gras* from the north by moonlight in his *bateau,* that carcajou, who doesn't care about borders, cannot travel here to govern the woods and the wild, to protect what is his?"

When Dubois uttered the word *smuggle,* he turned for the first time and looked directly at Cardonas, as if to affirm that he knew why a New York scientist might schedule an out-of-season pleasure trip to this remote wilderness. His look seemed to say, *We are one and the same.* Wulver was struck by the fact that gleaming above Dubois's ruddy, weathered nose, like two torches, were a blue eye on the left and a brown one on the right. It was an unforgettable face that suggested some kind of legendary provenance.

Wulver spoke again. "There are tales of wolverines bringing down disabled moose, elk, even buffalo. Animals five times their size."

Dubois took another puff. "Be careful on the lake, *mes amies.*"

Cardonas sighed to indicate that he was tired of the game. He walked down to the shore to mark up his map and examine the canoes. Dubois called after him.

"Elmwood, *mon frere!* Birch is for speed; elm is for strength. You will need the strong wood."

Dubois signaled with a nod for Wulver to follow him inside

the cabin. In the fireplace, embers were glowing against the October chill.

"I am taken for a full Quebecois because of my name and accent, but when the *couriers des bois* came three hundred years ago to send beaver pelts back to the hatters in Paris and London, there were no French women here. The trappers married, with or without the blessing of a priest, Iroquois women, *à la façon du pays*. Their children entered the tribal lineage, which comes down always from the mother. I am half French, half Iroquois. I was born up on the river, but I live here alone in the bush, with my brothers and sisters: the animals and trees. I need nothing."

He leaned in and lowered his voice, glancing down toward the put-in where Cardonas fussed about.

"I will give you something to guard your soul on the lake. When I passed from boyhood to manhood, in the North, I made my vision quest alone in the forest. When I returned to the long-house, the tribe saw that I was very strong. I began my training with the shaman. My body was already strong, but he taught me how to strengthen my soul. He taught me that the soul can travel. The soul can see at night. The soul is afraid of nothing, and when the soul needs more strength, it can reside in a stronger animal. If it needs to fly, it resides in the horned owl. If it needs to strip the bark off a tree, it resides in the bear, and if it needs to swim, it resides in the bullhead. The soul can inhabit the loon and dive, not just into the lake, but deep into the soul of the tribe, and see things that are not visible on the calm surface. The soul is the seat of power and wisdom." He paused. "I see that your soul is strong. I am near the end of my path. When you push off today, I will close the cabin, load the pelts in my *bateau*, and Jacques Dubois will make his last trip."

He paused again, reflecting.

"The shaman gave me this, and I promised that when I could

no longer use it, I would give it to another strong one. It has been handed down by the ancestors since the great ice melted back. It is from before the time of the Peacemaker, old as the ones who first came from the West. It must be handed on."

Dubois reached up to the mantel and took an object down. He handed it to Wulver. It was a hand-knapped stone spearhead. It was triangular, the size of a man's hand. Wulver recognized it as hecatolite, a type of feldspar. As Wulver turned it in his hands, the glinting light in the cabin made the stone's color shift from blue to opalescent pearl. Wulver recalled that the ancients believed the sorceress Hecate could turn moonbeams into this lustrous stone. The heft of the pointed weapon seemed to draw some kind of force from Floodwood Pond, and Wulver could feel it coursing through him.

"When you need help, and you will soon, keep this moonstone with you, and call to the governor, carcajou…" He broke off as Cardonas shouted from the lakeside.

"Gentleman, now spur the lated travelers apace!"

Dubois raised an eyebrow and spoke softly.

"Your companion quotes an assassin, *non? Prendre garde, mon ami.*"

The two men walked down to join Cardonas at the shoreline. Dubois waded in knee-deep, pushed the canoe free from shore, and steadied it while Cardonas and Wulver negotiated the gunwales and crouched over the keel to find their places. Once they were seated, he slipped the spearhead into Wulver's pack and hoisted the remaining gear onboard. He pushed them off and shouted, *"Au revoir, bon chance."* He watched them fall into their paddling rhythm, the younger man propelling in the bow, while the elder sat in the stern, using his paddle as a rudder. Dubois turned and walked back up to the cabin.

CHAPTER 5

THE LAKE

The two men made good time across the widest part of the lake, heading straight for a group of islands to the south. The Saint Regis wilderness was ideal for hunting and trapping, a fact that would have been well known to the Iroquois. Cardonas was becoming convinced that he would return with a stone weapon. He just had to find the right piece.

After twenty minutes of vigorous paddling, they reached the island complex. The two men began talking as they slowed their pace to survey the shorelines.

"Look around, Wulver. You are in the field now. You're not reading a book."

"I have seen much of this in books and in my imagination. I don't feel like a stranger here."

"Your imagination! So much for science, then. Let's go back in time and simply imagine, but not build, the wheel, the lever, concrete, electricity, and we'll see how far civilization progresses. Look here, Wulver. Head for that sandy point. We'll put down our first *baton rouge*."

Cardonas had packed a dozen wooden stakes, twelve inches in length with a sharpened point. Each one was painted red, with a bright white Strabo Society logo. They were issued by the club to explorers in order to lay claim to possible dig sites, and served as a sort of brand to warn curious interlopers that they were asking for trouble.

They spiked the first red stake, then spent the afternoon distributing the others around potential sites as they paddled from island to island. Migrating Canada geese honked overhead, and a kestrel swooped down to snare a lake trout in its talons. There was no sign all day of any inquisitive explorers who might be competing for archaeological glory.

The twelfth stake was put down around 5 p.m., as the sun was sinking behind the peaks to the west. The two men relaxed their pace, scouting for a camping spot. The islands dotting Floodwood were so small and numerous that most were not named, or in many cases even shown, on the map. Wulver thought of Melville: "It's not on any map. True places never are."

As the shadows of tall white pines spread over the glassy surface of the pond, the two explorers paddled slowly and retreated to their own inward meditations. Both were silent for a while.

Wulver broke the spell.

"Doctor Cardonas, have you ever read the Eastern scriptures on reincarnation?"

A great blue heron flushed from the cattails and flew overhead.

"My dear boy, we are here in the service of science, not superstition."

Wulver paddled for a while, then spoke again.

"The Eastern sages believe in the passage of our animating spirit into another creature, human or perhaps animal. Tell me, doctor, do you believe in the transmigration of souls?"

"Good god, man! What is this, a séance? Have we joined the

Theosophists? Where is the gypsy woman to tell our fortunes! What on earth has Van Leer been teaching you out there?"

The two men had become so involved in debate that they failed to notice a fallen tree that protruded from the bank of the island they were skirting. The canoe ground to a halt as it scraped the submerged trunk, and a dead branch, the kind lumberjacks call a widow-maker, swept along the keel line of the craft, missing both men but grabbing Wulver's pack, thrusting it momentarily into the air above their heads, and then dropping it back into the canoe. Wulver was pushing off on the submerged tree trunk with his paddle to free up the craft. He didn't see the spearhead roll out of his pack onto the keel.

Cardonas stared at the spearhead. He recognized the luster of hecatolite immediately. It had to be local. Wulver couldn't have brought it with him. And it was authentic Iroquois. Without leaving the canoe, he had found his grail. His mind raced. It would be no problem to concoct a report. The search, the digging, the clues, perhaps the bones of ancient game. The spearhead brought to the club, concealed in camping gear. Then the presentation to the Society, like a Roman triumph, and the award ceremony. The Strabo Medal! There was only one obstacle: Wulver. There would have to be a tragic accident, an overhanging limb. Wulver's inexperience. Cardonas's attempt to save him as the current carried him under. No witnesses.

Cardonas called forward to Wulver.

"Hard right! We'll put in by those rocks and make camp."

As they approached the rocks, still in six feet of water, Cardonas's paddle struck just once with enough force to throw the younger man overboard. He floated facedown while Cardonas counted two full minutes on his pocket watch. While he waited, Cardonas pulled the camping gear out of Wulver's pack and poled over to the rock pile. He filled the empty pack with rocks, strapped it on to Wulver, and let go. As his assistant, now his victim, disappeared, a great horned owl suddenly came screeching out of a towering white pine on shore. It went straight for Cardonas, who fended it off in a panic, struggling to keep the canoe from capsizing. He was crouching on the keel, the ribs digging into his knees, with his arms covering his head. Then the owl suddenly went quiet. After a few seconds, he heard the great wings as the bird flew off. The lake fell silent. Moving his arms away from his face, Cardonas reached down for the spearhead. It was gone.

The sun was going down. There was no chance to return to the outpost before dark. His arms were lacerated. There was nothing to do but tie the canoe to a branch of the spruce, wade onshore, and set up camp. He doused his arms with iodine, bellowing in pain. The owl answered from forty feet up in the pine. Cardonas managed to set up the tent. He would sleep until sunrise, then climb the tree if necessary to retrieve the spearhead. It was his. He committed a crime to take possession of it—a heinous crime, but that could be covered up. What's done is done. The important thing was to find the spearhead. When the darkness was complete, he doused the campfire and retired to his tent. As he secured his sleeping bag, he thought he heard a rustling in the brush outside. *Just my imagination…*

If any human had been within earshot of Cardonas's predawn cry for help, they would have missed it. It was covered up by the maniacal laugh of a loon, echoing across Floodwood Pond.

CHAPTER 6

REBIRTH

Wulver woke up. He could sense only panic. He didn't know who he was, where he was, or how he got there. He had no memory of who he might have been. He was lying on the ground, on a bed of pine needles. He turned his head and recognized shadowy things around him. Flowers, like gray five-pointed stars. He mouthed the word *asphodel* and fell back into a dreamless sleep. Hours or maybe days later, he heard a voice.

"Wulver."

Like the flowers, the name stirred something in his memory. The speaker was rubbing drops of oil under Wulver's nose. The powerful smell of musk flared his nostrils, and he opened his eyes. The speaker was standing over him. He wore a buckskin tunic and a bracelet of purple shells. Five bear claws hung on a rawhide thong around his neck. His face was painted with a slash of red ochre on one cheek and a slash of indigo on the other. His head was shorn except for a strip of jet-black hair bisecting his skull. The man had one blue eye, and one brown one. He gazed with an iron stare that looked past Wulver, who turned his head to follow it. They were both looking across a lake at high snow-capped peaks in the distance.

"Wulver. That is your name. Wulver."

He let that penetrate. He was in no hurry. The man gathered a handful of tobacco leaves from a woven basket and placed them in a rock circle. He struck his knife against a shard of flint and the sparks lit the dry tobacco. He spoke again.

"Wulver, you have traveled to the edge of the woods. This demands a ceremony of rebirth. I have rubbed you with the oil of your spirit animal. You must now be infused with Orenda, the life force. You are not all alive yet."

The man put one arm under Wulver's knees and the other arm behind his shoulders. He lifted the weak man effortlessly and walked toward the water. He deftly crossed the shoreline boulders on deerskin moccasins, and continued walking into the lake. He held Wulver at chest height, just above the waterline. He began to sing. He dipped Wulver under the surface once, twice, three times. He returned to the shore, placing Wulver back on his pine needle bed, and he sat with his back against a tall pine.

The weak man now understood that his name was Wulver. He began to know things. He knew what a tree was, and what the lake was. He knew that he was cold. He moved his limbs. The man attending him threw a fur pelt over him. He picked up a turtle shell and began to shake it. Pebbles inside the shell rattled in counterpoint as the man resumed singing. The shadow of the white pine covered their campsite, and darkness fell. Wulver closed his eyes and descended again, this time not into darkness, but into a dream.

In his dream, Wulver was moving through the forest, not on two legs, but on four. He brushed aside pine boughs with his head as he traveled rapidly. Sometimes he would stop at the water's edge and drink. He flushed a whitetail doe under a juniper and thought to give chase, but the moonlight was making him push onward. When the moon set behind the high peaks, he turned back. The narrow path was etched with five-clawed paw prints. As dawn spread her rosy fingers in the east, he found his bed beneath the boughs of the white pine. He opened his eyes. The man was standing over him, holding a wooden bowl and spoon.

"Eat."

Wulver was ravenously hungry. He opened his mouth like a baby bird, and the man spooned in cornbread soaked in maple syrup. When the bowl was empty, the man put it down and picked up a handful of ashes from the fire pit. He rubbed them on Wulver's forehead.

"You will begin to get stronger now."

The man sat cross-legged and faced Wulver squarely.

"You have been on your vision quest, Wulver. You have met your spirit animal. Your companion on the lake was treacherous, but your soul has traveled to a stronger place. You are a dead man, Wulver, but that is unimportant. We have performed the ceremony of birth."

Wulver tried speaking.

"Who are you?"

"My name is Deganawida. You knew me in your old life as Jacques Dubois. Generations ago, I was known as the Peacemaker. I united the five nations. Sky Woman, the creator of all, endowed me with the power that I passed on to you, the power of the stone spearhead."

He continued.

"Jacques Dubois is not a false name. In that body, I was Métis, both Iroquois and French. I know the ancient birch bark scrolls and I also know the words of Victor Hugo's 'Les Djinns.' There are djinns, magic beings, in this forest around us right now. I encompass many ages and many bodies. When I teach you, I am Deganawida."

He paused and closed his eyes.

"I have been on Floodwood since the great ice receded north. You are just beginning your journey as a shaman, Wulver. You have the spearhead that Sky Woman brought down from the moon, and you have traveled the old trail as your spirit animal."

He rose and went to the fire. He stirred a cast iron pot and spooned the contents onto a tin plate.

"These are the three sacred sisters that Sky Woman gave us. Corn, beans, and squash. We had great fields of these along the Mohawk River before your white-haired sachem gave the order to burn them and drive us north. We still grow them at Akwesasne, two days' walk north on the river. Eat and you will grow strong in body and spirit."

He handed the plate and spoon to Wulver, who fed himself until the tin was cleaned. Deganawida took the plate over the boulders and rinsed it in the lake. He shook the turtle shell again and sang a chant, looking out over the water. He returned and sat cross-legged once again.

"Wulver, do you recall Lethe Van Leer?"

A picture arose in Wulver's strengthening memory. He was crossing rolling hills. He waded through a marsh clogged with high cattails. When he reached shallow open water, a man was waving him onward from a red canoe.

He climbed in, and they paddled together under a railroad bridge where a shallow creek branched off from the pond. As they traveled, the man told him the names of trees on the bank. He pointed out ducks and cormorants diving for the minnows that thronged the clear water, and he showed the boy where the glaciers had left massive granite boulders. A great blue heron burst from the brush and flew overhead.

In his vision, Wulver felt that everything was alive, even the rocks and the river itself, and he was not an onlooker. He was part of it as well. The older man, sitting in the stern, steered the canoe into a narrow inlet. A bald eagle was perched on a fallen log. The creature's yellow eyes, created to look down from the distant sky, pierced the canoeists like lightning bolts. The great bird slowly gathered its potential, then lifted off the log. It flew, not up to the clouds, but toward the canoe, and its wings enveloped the boy.

Wulver opened his eyes.

"Van Leer taught me things?"

"Van Leer prepared you for your vision quest, for the power of the spearhead."

"Was he my father?"

Deganawida pulled his bear claw necklace over his head and placed it around Wulver's neck.

"That's enough questions for now, Wulver. Sky Woman and I are your guides. When the moon is once again full, your animal soul will hunt in the forest. But *faites attention,* Wulver, you will be hunted as well."

Deganawida turned and vanished. A horned owl called, high in the white pine, and Wulver heard the beating of its great wings as it took flight over Floodwood.

CHAPTER 7

FIRST SNOW

Under the November full moon, Deganawida taught Wulver how to track game, and he taught him how to use his powerful limbs to swim from island to island so that the entire St. Regis wilderness would be his kingdom. Even the black bears, larger and heavier, melted back into the forest when the strong musk preceded his passage. As the moon cycle drew to a close, the mentor sat with his protégé watching the sunset, chanting an evensong. Afterward, they lit the tobacco smudge, and Deganawida spoke.

"We are surrounded here by the spruce and the great white pine, Wulver, but the oaks have lost their leaves, and the maples are preparing to make sap for us. Tomorrow it will snow. I will come at sunrise in the canoe, and we will overwater to the cabin that I built with my hatchet and bucksaw when I was Jacques Dubois."

The air was crisp and cold as they crossed to the north side of the lake. When they put in, Deganawida leapt out with the rope. He tied the canoe to a limb and then stood bolt upright, staring uphill at the cabin. He sniffed the air, and then silently motioned for Wulver to get down out of sight below the gunwales. He crouched and vanished. In the woods, the owl called and then flew from a spruce toward the cabin. He perched on the roof, then flew down to the porch and pushed the unlocked door open. Wulver waited. After several minutes, Deganawida came out and signaled for Wulver to come up the hill.

"They were here. The ones who hunt you. Their scent still lingers. Tonight is the first snow. They will be back when the ice breaks, but not before. You will be safe here while the snow is deep."

The two men lit a votive tobacco fire and chanted their thanks for safe passage.

"When the moon is full, Wulver, the lakes will be frozen and you will be able to portage great distances to hunt. You must keep in mind, Wulver, that your life is no longer the life you lived before. You will spend the winters here at the cabin, and you will roam the woods when the ice has thawed and the trees bear leaves. You must not venture from this wilderness, even as many seasons pass. Someday it may no longer be safe here, and on that day, perhaps years from now, I will return to guide you onward. Remember that Sky Woman was here before the great ice, and she slept under it, a mile deep, for many thousand years. Say a prayer to her every night when you venture out on the ice, and keep this above the fire."

He placed the stone spearhead on the mantel where Wulver had first seen it.

"No one will steal it. I will be guarding it, and you."

Deganawida walked down to the canoe, waded out next to it, then stepped in deftly and steered straight south across the wide lake. As darkness fell, the first flakes of snow began to fall, and Wulver carried tinder, kindling, and three birch logs into the cabin.

CHAPTER 8

THE CALL

Seasons passed on Floodwood. Under the full moon Wulver traversed the iced-over lakes, tracing the hopping tracks of snowshoe hare. He encountered bobcats, lynx, even a cougar, and they all backed off and disappeared into the shadows. When the ice cracked and roared in the spring, he would desert the cabin and haunt the woods and the wild, watching hunters and campers from the dark, as they sat around their fire circles, telling ghost stories. Little did they know...

And thus forty cycles of Nature passed.

During the long nights of the new moon, Wulver sat very still, recalling everything he had read when alive, when Van Leer was preparing him. He could recite bits of Plato and Aristotle, and passages from Virgil's *Aeneid*. The Latin rolled off his tongue and gave him great pleasure. Most of all, he loved reciting, word for word, passages from the Heart Sutra, the ancient Buddhist teaching on reincarnation. It was comforting to Wulver to know that he was not alone in the universe. There were others before him, and there would be others after him. He kept Deganawida's counsel and was wary of humans. Despite his previous brotherhood with them, he knew that they would view him with horror, and his vision quest would be abrogated.

One night, as the flames leapt up below the heavy oak mantel, he fixed his eyes on the fire, and a vision came to him.

An old man was reading a book. It was Lethe Van Leer. In the flames, Van Leer closed the book and raised his head to face his stepson.

"Alistair, it is now forty years since you left Acheron, indeed since you left this life and took solitary refuge in the great forest. I know that you are alive now in a greater way than when I brought you to my house and raised you as a son. You live now as both man and animal. In death you have forged the ultimate bond with Nature. I understand that, and the old ones who first hunted the forest understood, but there are many outside of the woods who do not understand, and what they don't understand they seek to destroy. They are already hunting you. That is all that I can tell you while the flames burn down, Alistair. Beware. You will not see me again. You will come here where you were raised, the place you see in dreams, after the snow. The great house will be gone. I have placed my books, your books now, in the gatehouse, the place I call Graymalkin House. You will come here, and you will be home, but you will not be safe. I wish it could be otherwise. Goodbye, Alistair."

The flames died down to embers, and Wulver slept.

When the ice broke out on the lake, Wulver saw the canoe coming. Deganawida sat with him and they chanted, welcoming spring, with frosty breath. Then Deganawida spoke.

"After all these years, it is no longer safe for you to be here, Wulver. The lake has thawed once again. The road will be clear soon, and the logging train will begin running once more, belching the sparks that set the forest on fire. You must leave before you become prey. The horned owl will guide you south. Travel the ridges by night and keep the North Star, the drinking gourd, at your back. When you reach the widest part of the great river, there is a gap in the high cliffs. You must cross there, as a man by daylight, or a beast by moonlight. From there I will guide you to Graymalkin House. Depart tonight, and pack the stone spearhead with you. Safe journey, my…"

He hesitated.

"My son."

CHAPTER 9

THE HOUSE WITH NO ADDRESS

October 1960, Westchester County, New York

A thick fog was rolling off the Ramapo range, stealing across the Hudson. It was beginning to envelop Route 9 as Detective Sergeant Kevin Macduff nursed his unmarked patrol car north. It was not yet 8 p.m., but the late October sun had sunk below the mountains two hours earlier, and the dense mist was starting to reflect Macduff's headlight beams back into his eyes. By the time he reached North Tarrytown and turned west down the hill into Sleepy Hollow, the black Ford Interceptor was crawling slowly, while Macduff kept an eye out for deer.

Deer were part of the reason he was cruising Route 9. There had been a recent spate of deer slain in the lower Hudson valley, not just on the road but also in the woods and fields, and lately the problem was extending to sheep. Farmers and old-timers were suggesting that a predatory beast, perhaps a wolf, had taken up residence in the hills surrounding the usually peaceful village of Tarrytown.

Macduff was feeling a bit sleepy as he crept through the lowland fog. This wasn't his beat, and Route 9's local name, Broadway, belied its dark and winding two lanes. He was crossing the bridge by the old Philipse Manor when a banshee-like shriek shattered the veil of quiet that laid over the dark hollow. Momentarily, the hair on the back of his neck stiffened, and he caught his breath. "Of course. It's the firehouse, calling volunteers." He'd passed the Union Hose Company just a mile back. Macduff settled back into piloting the Ford as he passed the Old Dutch Cemetery.

Kevin Macduff didn't believe in banshees. He was a cop. Perhaps a distant Celtic ancestor had possessed the second sight, the ability to see and communicate with ghosts, fairies, and so forth, but Kevin didn't inherit that gene, and he was glad for it. A law enforcement graduate of Fordham, his job left no room for selkies, kelpies, brownies, or any other superstitious concoctions of his ancestors. On this particular evening, though, he was searching for a house with no address.

CHAPTER 10

THE SOCIETY

Two weeks earlier, Macduff's chief, Sean O'Malley, had given him a piece of interesting news. The Strabo Society was interested in talking to him. Charles Iverson, the director of the famed but secretive geographers' club, had contacted Westchester headquarters, requesting a meeting with a discreet investigator. Everything would be off the record. The chief was on the club's annual banquet guest list, and it was understood that he would take care of everything needed should a request from the Society come over his desk.

He advised Macduff to leave the uniform and badge in his locker and wear a necktie and sport coat. The club, located on New York's Upper East Side, had a strict dress code, and a uniformed policeman would raise eyebrows. The meeting was scheduled for noon on October 20, in the library. The room was paneled in ponderous oak, and men talked quietly over maps and thick leather volumes. It took a few seconds to adjust his eyes to the dark. A man at a corner table waved him over.

Iverson was a veteran. He'd made his bones in the field, dodging arrows in a dugout canoe on the Amazon and driving a Jeep across the Gobi Desert in search of a mastodon skull. Once, in the Hindu Kush, he was kidnapped by hashish smugglers and held in a dungeon in Kashmir until a satchel full of cash arrived to ransom him. The address on the satchel simply read "Skull and Bones Society, Yale University."

Iverson shook Macduff's hand vigorously. He wore a Harris tweed shooting jacket over a button-down shirt. His tie was navy blue, with the Yale "open book" shield logo. He beckoned for Macduff to sit down. Before he spoke, he dragged his meerschaum pipe through a pouch of St. Bruno Flake, tamped the bowl, and lit it. He shook the match and dropped it on the floor. He puffed twice and then took a deep draft.

"From the Owl Shop, of course. Tell me, Macduff, do you smoke?"

"No sir."

"Pity. But let's get down to business. Do you know the name Alistair Wulver?"

"No. Geographer?"

"He was indeed a geographer, and he still may be, for all we know. Here, take a look at this."

Iverson tossed a manila envelope across the table. It contained only three items. The first was on Strabo Society letterhead, dated October 20, 1920, exactly forty years to the day prior to the present moment. It read:

Mission: Search for evidence of Iroquois hunting in St. Regis wilderness. Return artifacts along with full report to Society director.
Location: All research to take place within Adirondack State Park.
Eyes only: No permits. Artifacts carried out in camping gear.
Party: Anthony Cardonas (leader) Alistair Wulver (assistant).

The second item was a bill on St. Regis House Hotel letterhead. It read:

Cardonas/Wulver party checked in October 27, 1920.
Left hotel same day in hired car.
Did not return to collect personal belongings or check out.
$112 charged to Strabo Society running account.

"So these two left forty years ago and neither has been heard
from since?"
"Until last Friday. Read the third item."
It was last week's *Tarrytown Daily News* dated October 14,
opened to the editorial page. A letter to the editor was circled.
It read:

Dear Sirs:

In regard to your recent reporting on the "mysterious" local slaying
of deer, rabbits, and other woodland creatures, as well as domestic
sheep, it's not a mystery at all, and your characterization of it
as such only reveals your human-centric ignorance of natural
processes. Animals eat to survive. Must I point out your own
appetite for beef, pork, and lamb? Undoubtedly we have a local
resident, perhaps a wolf, a bear with a taste for meat, or something
more exotic that we haven't managed to extinguish yet. Would
you cringe at the notion that a lynx or even a cougar had traveled
from a far-off wilderness to your idyllic village? It would be
easy work for such a creature to move undetected through the
Adirondacks, Catskills, and Ramapos. All that would remain
would be to hitch a ride on a late-night cargo ferry across the
river. If you have any knowledge of natural history, and I have
no certainty that you do, you know that our esteemed main road,
which we pretentiously refer to as Broadway, was a throughway
for native peoples for millennia, and before that a well traveled

riverside path for every variety of animal, from salamanders to dire wolves, dating back to the retreat of the glaciers. I beg you to look at this situation from the animal's point of view, if you have the magnanimous spirit within you to do so, and make room for him, as he has been forced to make room for us. If I am correct about the existence of this creature, and I believe I am, then he is simply fulfilling his role in the eternal drama of Nature, without judgment or rancor. Can the same be said about man?

Sincerely,

Alistair Wulver
Graymalkin House
Scarborough

Iverson lowered his voice.

"That ran last Thursday. I responded with a letter to the editor that went up on Saturday. On Monday Wulver posted this."

He handed Macduff a page from Monday's paper.

If a Strabo man knocks on my door at 9 p.m. on November 3, I will receive him. I have a story to tell, while there is still time.

"Of course, he doesn't give us a clue to exactly where Graymalkin House is, except that if he's telling the truth, it's in Scarborough, out past Tarrytown."

Macduff frowned and scratched his head. His tousled hair was crimson, the color of the October maple leaves in Central Park, just down the block from the club.

"So I don't just find him, I have to find the house too. It certainly is curious."

"It's more than curious, Macduff. Two men went out on assignment for the Society. Neither returned. Now one has resurfaced, four decades later. He deliberately made himself known, and he is the only one who can tell us what happened up there.

I'm sending you to find out the truth. I will be listed as mission leader, but you will go alone. I will notify Wulver in the letters to the editor and tell him you are coming. You understand that you will be in civilian clothes, identifying yourself as a member of the Strabo Society. Report back directly to me and no one else. Chief O'Malley has been briefed on all of this. No word to the press, the mayor, or anyone else. This is a mysterious business, and it stays strictly within the Society. Understood?"

"Of course. A discreet errand."

"If you're lucky, Macduff, an errand is all it will be." He rose, and they shook hands.

"Just one more question. Exactly where am I going?"

"I wish I could tell you precisely. Graymalkin House is rumored to be the gatehouse of the demolished Acheron Hall. It's somewhere along the river side of Route 9 in Scarborough, as you head north from Tarrytown. Lethe Van Leer, who built it to house his taxidermy collection, was a Yale man, a founding member of the Strabo Society, and a Shakespeare buff with a taste for the occult. It was his idea to call the gatehouse Graymalkin House. Something to do with Shakespeare. He vanished, and the big house was torn down. No one seems to know who owns the property now, and any record of the estate's former location seems to have vanished. The millionaires along that stretch didn't bother with street addresses back in the Gilded Age. Apparently our man has been living in the abandoned gatehouse, sans the trappings of modern life, for god knows how long. Good luck, Macduff. Did I mention that you should carry a concealed sidearm?"

CHAPTER 11

GRAYMALKIN HOUSE

Macduff's black cruiser crept north on Route 9. A few miles past the Dutch Cemetery, the mist parted just enough for him to make out a street sign, leading downhill toward the river: Revolutionary Road. The act of glancing at it took his eyes off Broadway for a split second, and when he looked back, a creature the size of a small black bear was crouched on the road, directly in his path. The Ford's headlights picked up a set of fangs locked in a snarl, and a pair of blazing yellow eyes. Macduff instinctively slammed on the brake pedal as he swerved into the oncoming lane, coming to rest on the far shoulder. On a foggy night there was no local traffic heading southbound, so car and driver were unscathed. There was no further sign of the creature, save for a pungent musky odor. Macduff collected himself and glanced at his new surroundings. The car was aimed downhill on a gravel driveway, facing a massive stone archway. Through the ivy and trumpet vine covering the structure, he could make out a word etched in Latin-style letters: ACHERON.

The driveway was overgrown with weeds, but passable. Macduff had only to locate the gatehouse. At that moment, the fog lifted, revealing a full autumn moon, and in the sudden bluish light he got his first glimpse of Graymalkin House. The stone structure, like the gate it once guarded, was covered in ivy and vines. It looked more like a ruin than a dwelling. It was surrounded by a copse of some kind of exotic willow. As Macduff turned the Ford's ignition key, he thought momentarily of a line from Shakespeare. The third witch whom Macbeth encounters in the forest ends their meeting by rejoining her familiar, the cat that she inhabits, uttering the words "I come, Graymalkin."

Macduff shook his shoulders to compose himself, banishing any literary or even fantastical notions. It did seem, though, that the animal on the road somehow directed him to this lonely spot. He was on an assignment, though, and he needed his wits about him. Collect the data—in this case the old man's story—and report back to Iverson. Steady on.

The driveway continued downhill toward the bluff where the old mansion must have stood. Beyond that was the river. Macduff drove slowly toward the house. The place looked uninhabited, and despite the Ford's clock reading 9 p.m., his appointed time, the windows were dark, save one candle glowing toward the rear of the building. Macduff climbed the front steps and knocked loudly on the heavy oak door. There was no response from within. He heard a rustle in the low-hanging willows, and a twig snapped. He ignored the hairs rising once again on the back of his neck and walked gingerly through a sea of weeds toward the back of the house. An ancient Ford Model A touring car was parked there. In the moonlight it looked like a rusty, ivy-covered Sphinx.

As he pulled out his notebook and pen to sketch a map of the scene, the candlelit window went dark. The adjacent window was illuminated next, and then that went dark. The sequence was leading toward the front door. Macduff pocketed his notebook and walked around to the front to meet his interview subject.

CHAPTER 12

THE OCCUPANT

"Mr. Macduff, I presume? Iverson informed me that you would be coming."

"That's correct, sir. Pleased to meet you."

Macduff extended a hand, which the older man ignored.

"Alistair Wulver. Come in. I have things to tell you."

Macduff followed the elderly man's candle through two ante-rooms. Wulver wore a knee-length black wool coat, and his gait was surprisingly graceful and lithe, almost feline. The third room was Wulver's study. He motioned for Macduff to sit down. He placed the candle on a small table. It was the only light in the room, and apparently the only light in the entire house. The two men sat facing each other. Wulver spoke first.

"You are wondering if I live here alone."

He gestured toward the bookshelves that lined three walls of the small chamber.

"By no means! I live with these, my lifelong companions. Look at the names, Macduff. It is Macduff, isn't it? Plato, Aristotle, Sophocles. Tell me, my young inquisitor, have you read and taken to heart these ancient texts?"

"To be honest, sir, I took some liberal arts courses at Fordham, but I didn't really concentrate on the classics."

Wulver sighed.

"Then what you have learned, young man, is pablum, predigested by sophists who crawl about the dark corners of Plato's cave, take a few measurements, and then give each other awards, celebrating with Champagne toasts. Fools."

He was silent for a moment. Then he fixed Macduff again with his piercing gaze. "Tell me something, Macduff. Are you familiar with Hermeticism, St. Germain, the dicta of Pythagoras concerning the transmigration of souls?"

Macduff realized that any questions he had prepared were not going to find purchase. In the candle flame, he had a momentary dreamlike vision of the Ford Interceptor drifting out into the Hudson, with him at the wheel, unable to stop it. He shook his head and blinked.

"To be honest, sir, I don't recognize those names."

"Then what I tell you tonight will have no meaning, but time is short, so I must begin. Should you return to the club, you must tell Iverson that you saw me, and I was unquestionably alive. Do you understand?"

Macduff did not understand, but he bit his lower lip and said, "Yes."

Wulver closed his eyes, and seemed to fall asleep. The candle cast dancing shadows on the book-lined walls, and Macduff thought he heard the old man purr softly, like a napping cat. After several minutes, Wulver's eyes reopened. He no longer looked at Macduff. He stared straight into the candle, as if the flame itself was generating a story that he would narrate from a distance, in the third person. When he spoke, it was in the detached voice of a man under hypnosis. He began.

CHAPTER 13

A STRANGE TALE

"The Strabo Society of today…"

He paused, as if turning a page in his mind.

"The Strabo Society of today bears little resemblance to the vision of its founders. They were men of insight as well as eyesight. They could gather evidence by meditating in silence. They could see outside Plato's cave, and they knew the true meaning of alchemy, which has little to do with chemicals.

"Lethe Van Leer, who built Acheron Manor, trained a young protégé in subjects that are not taught in the Ivy League. Some of his own books rest behind me now."

Macduff glanced up at the back wall. A stone spearhead rested on one of the oak shelves. The dusty books perched like vultures. He shook off another feeling of dread.

"He gathered knowledge from books, but also from the woods, from the rocks left by the glaciers, and from the great birds that hunt on the Croton and the Pocantico rivers. When his student was ready, Van Leer brought him to the Society. It was 1920, the old club on the west side, near the museum. Sinclair ran the show back then. He was a man whose vision would make your microscope seem like a child's toy, but he couldn't tell the future, so he didn't know what would happen when he sent the young initiate on his test assignment with Anthony Cardonas. Or perhaps he did know."

He chuckled, ruefully.

"Oil and water. There was no alchemy in that compound. Cardonas was an empiricist; he only believed in what he could see, what he could prove. Above all, Cardonas was a politician. To him, the society was a stepping-stone. His goal was the Strabo Medal, given, as you know, for significant discovery in cultural anthropology. After that, he would be in a position to lobby the club's wealthy donors for his own advantage. A museum curatorship would lead to election to city government, and from there he could amass not only wealth but power as well. The study of geography was of little consequence to him, and he would stop at nothing to achieve his goal. Never was there a two-man team, politician and mystic, more mismatched."

As the candle burned, Wulver spun the tale of the trip to Floodwood, about Dubois, the great white pines, and the horned owl. Wulver described his own murder, his transmigration to a savage beast, and the retribution that fell on his killer, followed by his own redemption and initiation into the mystical life of the shaman. Finally, as the bell of St. Mary's chapel on the Woodlea estate across Route 9 rang twelve times, Wulver fell silent.

The candle had burned almost all the way down. Macduff had been scribbling for three full hours while Wulver told his bizarre tale. Now it was too dark to review his notes, but he knew one thing. He couldn't present a work of pure fiction, told by a madman, to Iverson. Macduff's instruction was to be polite and make no attempt to engage in debate, no matter how far-fetched the old man's story might be, but he couldn't resist.

"With all due respect, sir, my assignment was to gather a report on a Strabo expedition, not relay a ghost story, although it certainly was worthy of Irving or even Poe."

"So, young man, you think my life—or, more properly, lives are a work of fiction?"

Macduff kept his eyes on his notebook, in a posture of defense. As he waited for a reply, the fog parted again and the room was flooded with moonlight.

There was no sound for several minutes except heavy, labored breathing. Then Macduff heard a low growl. He kept his head down, trying to delay the fight-or-flight response, but the hair on the back of his neck stiffened once more. Then he smelled it; the overwhelming musk. In the last flicker of the candle, Kevin Macduff raised his head and stared directly into a pair of blazing yellow eyes.

There was no time to reach for his .38. Macduff crashed through the leaded glass window and raced to his car. His hands shook, but he managed to turn the ignition key. He backed through the archway and sped north on Route 9. His red hair had gone white. He didn't stop until he reached his uncle's farm in the Catskills.

Ten days later, Iverson jotted a note on Strabo Society letterhead. It read:

Mission: Interview Alistair Wulver re: 1920 Cardonas/Wulver expedition.

Location: Graymalkin House, exact location tbd; Scarborough, N.Y.?

Party: Charles Iverson (leader) Kevin Macduff (assistant).

Eyes only: Macduff failed to return or file report. Case remains open.

Iverson slipped the note into a manila envelope and dropped it into his file cabinet. He locked the carbon copy in a leather pouch and ordered it to be hand-delivered at once to an address on the east end of Long Island.

The next afternoon, Iverson's office phone rang. It was Duncan Sinclair, Iverson's mentor and predecessor as director of the Society. He was a legendary geographer and explorer. His name was spoken in hushed tones by his colleagues. On the phone, he was a man of few words.

"Chuck, I have information that you need to move forward. Be at my place in Sag Harbor at four tomorrow. Come alone."

CHAPTER 14

THE MEETING

Iverson cursed the traffic. Getting across the 59th Street Bridge was bad enough, but the snarl of Queens traffic heading for Idlewild was threatening to make him late for his meeting. Iverson did not like being thrown off schedule. He grumbled out loud to his otherwise empty Buick.

"Damn it, Sinclair is likely to be *non compos mentis* by the time I get there, if he's already started on his afternoon whiskey and water."

Traffic eased up after Massapequa, and by the time he crossed the bridge onto the South Fork, he was practically alone on the road in off-season Southampton. He passed the pumpkin fields, going to seed in the late autumn chill. He slowed down as he pulled into Bridgehampton, looking for the left turn that would take him into Sag Harbor. Duncan Sinclair's place was surrounded by an eight-foot boxwood hedge. At eighty years old, with much of it spent in dangerous situations around the world, he liked his privacy.

Iverson handed off his jacket to Ewan, Sinclair's valet and bodyguard. He was shown to a glass-walled room at the rear of the rambling house. Sinclair sat reading the Sunday *Times*, a manila folder on his lap. He wore a bulky knit sweater with an embroidered chenille patch depicting the Yale bulldog leaning pugnaciously on the letter *Y*. In retirement, he'd taken the liberty to grow a white beard, which might have been out of fashion in his heyday, roaring twenties New York City, but was now entirely fitting for an intrepid old explorer. Iverson noted that the whiskey bottle on the table was only about a third empty. Good. It wasn't a social visit. The older man motioned for him to sit.

"Duncan, I suppose we both know why I've driven all the way out here."

"This business with Wulver and Cardonas. It never went away, did it?"

"Well, if it did, it's back."

"How much do you know?"

After forty years, Iverson was well aware that when his mentor asked that question, he already knew more than Iverson did. Sinclair was elderly and slowing down, but his investigative mind was still firing on all cylinders.

"Damn little, Duncan. That's the issue."

"Chuck, we can speak freely here. This goes back to Van Leer. He was a thorn in the side of the Society, and when he brought in the lad Wulver, he was attempting to plant a new thorn to succeed him. He was a major donor and a charter member, a founder, so I had to accommodate him. My feeling then was that the boy was not right for the club. He had been inculcated with Van Leer's mystical bent, and at the time it seemed like a threat."

"At the time...You don't think that now?"

"We'll get to that. At the time, as you say, I half expected only one man to return from Floodwood. I knew Cardonas and

I knew his temperament. Let's leave it at that. I did not expect both men to disappear from the face of the earth."

"I reread the file when I sent Macduff out for the interview. Like something straight out of Arthur Conan Doyle. And now Macduff has disappeared too.'

"Yes. The detective you sent out to Westchester. Chuck, I read that letter to the Tarrytown newspaper. I was Wulver's mentor, as I was yours, and I will swear to you that it was indeed written by him."

Sinclair filled his tumbler halfway with water and topped it off from his whiskey bottle.

"The Glenlivet, Chuck. Straight from Josie's Well, Speyside."

He took a draft, eyes closed.

"Care for a dram of the *aqua vitae*, Chuck?"

"No thanks. I've got a ninety-mile drive home, and besides, I've got a mystery to solve."

"Tell me something, Chuck. When you mentioned Conan Doyle, were you thinking perhaps of the Hound of the Baskervilles?"

Iverson snorted.

"Figure of speech, Duncan. That's all."

Sinclair beckoned for the younger man to pull his chair closer. He lowered his voice.

"Something strange happened at Floodwood, and I fear it may have happened again out in Scarborough."

He took another quaff. The shadows were growing longer.

"What I am going to tell you will cause you to think me senile, but I guarantee that I can still back-rank checkmate you in a dozen moves. Listen to me, Chuck. I've seen much since the early days of the Society, everything short of the damned giant rat of Sumatra. This business is different from anything I've encountered, but it brings to mind various long-held beliefs in certain cultures."

Iverson didn't answer. He knew Sinclair would continue.

"The men vanished in late October 1920. I knew then that by the end of November the entire St. Regis region would be covered in snow five feet deep, and it would stay like that until April. As the club director, I considered it urgent to find evidence quickly."

"Of a crime?"

"Of whatever. We had no clues, no witnesses. It's a wilderness. I contacted the hotel and they discreetly retained a trustworthy guide to comb the area by canoe. If they put down Strabo red stakes, it might be possible to trace their path."

He paused.

"All right, Chuck, go ahead and ask."

"Okay. Did he find anything?"

"A few stakes, yes. That was all. The following day he took a ride up to the Akwesasne reservation and asked around. An Iroquois hunter by the name of Kariwase had come across odd things out on the islands. The next morning they put out from Floodwood Cabin. There was no sign of Dubois, the outfitter. Kariwase paddled to a remote island on the south end of the lake. There were the remains of a campsite. One of Dubois's rental tents, two Strabo Society backpacks, one filled with rocks, the other empty except for Cardonas's wallet, cash intact."

"Was that all?"

"No. They found bones, picked clean and scattered about. Some crunched in pieces. Had to be the work of a powerful predator."

"A rogue black bear, Duncan. They'll eat anything in November."

"There were tracks. Five claws like a bear, but a smaller print. Kariwase identified them. Wolverine."

"Good god, Duncan. That far south of the Saint Lawrence?"

Sinclair shrugged.

"We can't control a wild animal's range. We just pretend that we can."

"Anything else?"

"They searched the area. They found the tracks of both men, but it was puzzling. One man tracked from a white pine where the torn canoe rope was still hanging. No canoe in sight. That track went to the fire pit and from there to the tent, also badly torn."

"And the second man?"

"Damned strange. His track came straight out of the water about twenty yards away from the other, and led directly into a buckthorn thicket."

"And they exited where?"

"They didn't. The thicket is where the wolverine tracks first appear. They emerge, circle the tent, and then we have the mayhem. From there they led to the broken rope, the canoe tie-up."

"So the bones are the bones of just one of the men?"

"Correct."

"And you say the second man's tracks led to the canoe?"

"No. The wolverine's."

Iverson struggled not to show what he was thinking.

"Duncan. With all due respect, wolverines don't paddle canoes. Are you suggesting that an accomplice spirited the creature away in a canoe? This is not making any sense."

"Allow me to continue, Chuck. Kariwase reported other sites in Floodwood with similar man-to-wolverine tracks. I can tell you what he surmised."

"This isn't a German fairy tale, is it, Duncan?"

"No. It's an Iroquois belief. When I read the report forty years ago I dismissed it as superstition, a dead end. I filed it and tried to forget it. I went on expeditions, ran the society, retired here to my oyster farm, but I never forgot. Then we have this letter to the editor signed by Wulver, and a missing detective."

He took a sip from his tumbler.

"Before you respond, Chuck, hear me out. I not only have seen but also have learned much over the years, not inside the walls of the club but in the field, where I found myself immersed in so-called primitive cultures. Those people may not be scientists, but they have survived through the ages without the destructive trappings of 'civilization,' the weaponry I saw deployed in the Great War, and you saw in the next one. I learned to listen to the shamans. We may call them savage, but what would they say about Dresden, Hiroshima, the near extinction of this continent's native population?"

Sinclair paused, took a deep breath and sighed.

"I learned to respect their body of knowledge just as I respect Aristotle, Lucretius, and Newton. If the Iroquois believe that the soul can migrate from one creature to another—and in this particular case, it's the only possible explanation that we have—then I am inclined to believe them."

"So we're looking for a werewolf, then? Or should I say a were-wolverine?"

"We're not. She is."

Sinclair pulled a business card from his vest pocket and handed it to Iverson. It read:

Artemis Fletcher
Arbalist

The address was a mailbox at Sarah Lawrence College in Bronxville, Westchester.

"It's not her first job for us, Chuck. Give her free rein and let me know what she reports. May I remind you of the secrecy that must surround this? The Strabo Society annual donors banquet is coming up on New Year's Day, and we can't have the high rollers whispering about murder and mayhem within the society's ranks while they dine on their wild boar Provençal. Any questions?"

"Just one. If there exists a report submitted by Kariwase and the guide, why wasn't it in my file when I took over the director-ship of the club?"

Sinclair patted the manila folder on his lap and smiled.

"Surely, Chuck, you know that there is 'eyes only,' and then there is the 'eyes only' above that. Ewan will fetch your jacket. You should be able to pick up the new expressway at Jericho. Good luck, Chuck."

CHAPTER 15

THE HUNTRESS

Artemis Fletcher was winding up her Wednesday lecture hall class.

"Reports on Richard the Second and the Peasant Revolt are due on Friday, double spaced. And don't forget, much as we all love Shakespeare, he wrote drama, not medieval history, so choose your sources carefully."

Tall, athletic, and blond, with a Nordic aspect, Professor Fletcher could easily be mistaken for one of her college-age students. She zipped her black leather Schott jacket and hiked across campus to the history department. Before leaving for home on Mondays, Wednesdays, and Fridays, she made it a habit to check her inbox at the office one last time. On this particular Wednesday, there was an envelope bearing the Strabo Society emblem. She thought back to the trip up the Amazon basin, the grizzly episode on Kodiak Island, and especially the job outside of the village of Agincourt in France, where she fired her bolts from the hillside where Henry V's longbowmen, the band of brothers, stood their ground.

Artemis combined her interest in medieval history with actual practice. As a world champion crossbow competitor, she had used her arm muscles like a concert pianist to defeat target shooters, mostly male, from around the world. Her father, Alcon Fletcher, a champion himself, had put a scaled-down tiller in her hands when she was old enough to walk, and by the time she was in her mid-teens, she had bagged her African "big five."

It was only when her aim was slightly off on a single shot on the Veldt and she saw the ensuing torment of a wounded animal that she felt a true empathy with the creatures she had been hunting, and she retired from tracking big game. By age twenty-eight she had won every world title, and she constrained her crossbow work to target practice on her estate, Atalanta in Valhalla, Westchester County. With no need to train for tournaments, she was free to study Leonardo's designs and experiment with her own innovative triggers and bolts. Her specialty was the modernization of the arbalest, the super-weapon of the twelfth century. Of course, when the CIA needed a minefield swept, or if Duncan Sinclair, an old friend of her father's, needed a surreptitious crossbow mission, she was not averse to an adventure, by any means.

She was familiar with the name Charles Iverson, Sinclair's successor at the Strabo directorship. She read the particulars and reflected ruefully for a moment that the Society was willing to hire her for secret missions that were deemed too dangerous for club members, but as a woman, she wouldn't even be allowed in the front door of the building unless it was to pony up a donation at the annual banquet. The details of this one looked interesting, though. Iverson gave her what scant details he knew. The subject was Alistair Wulver, a scientist who disappeared four decades earlier. It was suspected that he might be hiding out in Westchester County, at a place called Graymalkin House on the grounds of an abandoned estate that was known as Acheron. No one seemed to know exactly where it was, but a recent clue indicated that his den might be there. Iverson used the word *den* without irony, and he instructed her to search wooded areas under the full moon for five-clawed wolverine tracks. His careful wording avoided the term *werewolf*, but she got the gist. Her interest was piqued. This fellow, or creature, was thought to have traveled from a lair deep in the Adirondacks all the way downriver to Westchester. If that was true, she would be tracking it somewhere within a few miles of her own home. As a historian, she considered herself a rational scholar, not given to belief in monsters, but as an adventurer, she kept an open mind whenever a new challenge was presented, and this was certainly new.

Friday, December 2, was her last class before semester break, so she had two weeks to grade papers, train back up to championship level on her backyard targets, and research old German folk tales for clues as to how to track the creature. She had dealt with those grizzlies on Kodiak Island, a ghostly snow leopard in Sichuan Province, and a nest of king cobras in Bengal, but this would be entirely different.

On the third of December, Artemis packed a Westchester trail map in her hunting kit, along with a newly designed small crossbow that she could conceal unnoticed in a duffel bag. It wouldn't do to wander through the peaceful river towns shouldering a medieval weapon.

Artemis loaded the gear onto the rear deck of her Willys Jeep. On the map, she highlighted all the areas in the county where a creature could move by night, undetected. There was no shortage of wooded parkland in the area. She began the search before dawn, driving Route 9 from Lyndhurst Castle in Irvington north all the way to the Putnam County border. Had she taken a closer look at a decrepit stone archway on the left as she passed through Scarborough, she might have noticed the engraved ACHERON, overgrown with vines, and a single candle burning in the rear window of a rundown gatehouse.

Her perimeter marked out, she took the afternoon off to read her highlighted sections of Ortega y Gasset's *Meditations on Hunting*. The next move, after dark, was to zero in on specific heavily wooded areas. One of them, the forest extending east from the Kensico Reservoir, was so close to her Atalanta estate that she left the Jeep in her garage and hiked into the woods with her miner's headlamp on. The duffel bag containing her cross-bow and bolts was over her shoulder. She started scanning for tracks at the base of the Kensico Dam. Crossing Route 22, she followed an old rail bed through the woods toward Cranberry Lake. A purpose-built short rail line had once led from the dam construction area to a granite quarry a mile east. Stone was cut there and loaded onto rolling stock for cartage to the site, where it was formed into blocks and hoisted into place by ten-ton over-head cranes. Loose scraps of rock were mixed with quick-drying cement and poured as concrete. After the completion of the mas-sive structure, the rails were pulled up and the quarry was aban-doned, eventually filling with rainwater as forest reclaimed the surroundings.

Artemis walked slowly, following her headlamp beam, look-ing for tracks, scat, broken branches—anything to indicate that a short but muscular animal had passed. As she reached the old quarry, the full moon emerged from behind a cloud bank, reveal-ing a landscape that wouldn't have looked out of place on the lunar surface itself, save for the blackwater pond that filled the lower depth of the pit. The projecting stones formed hillocks and towering cairns that suggested a moonlit gothic cathedral. She jumped, catlike, from boulder to boulder, still the wary hunter but recalling teenage hikes to the quarry under the full moon. A glint in a stone crevice caught her eye. The moonlight had caught the sparkle of a particularly lustrous stone, wedged into a crack in what appeared to be a cave entrance. She pulled the stone out. As a literal fletcher, a maker of arrows, she recognized right away that it was a spearhead. The glint was a clue that it might be moonstone, something normally found up north in the Adirondacks. It was too carefully placed to be an ancient glacial erratic. Someone, or something, had put it there. Was it a signpost, a warning to intruders, a talisman? The cave entrance was too small to admit Artemis, but a strong smell of musk hung in the air. She sat silently for fifteen minutes, watching and listening. If this was indeed the creature's lair, he was abroad, probably hunting in the moonlight. The granite boulders didn't reveal tracks. She decided to retrace her steps, but first she dropped the stone into her duffel bag.

Halfway back toward Route 22, she passed a trail junction that led a few yards to an old root cellar that locals called the stone chamber. It was there that she found the tracks. They showed five claws like a bear, but without a bear's heavy pad impression. Like most hikers in the lower forty-eight states, she had never seen an actual wolverine print, but she knew what to look for, and this was it. The creature must have been denned in the stone chamber, which means she walked within a few yards of it as she made her way into the woods. Now she could detect the scent of musk. The game was afoot.

The tracks led west on the rail bed, toward the dam. Artemis took a deep breath and followed. When she reached the flat spillway beneath the twelve-story massif, the animal's tracks led onto the concrete terrace that surrounded a reflecting pool. The creature must have stopped to drink at the moon's reflection. The concrete surface made it impossible to stalk its path onward. She decided to climb the stairs to the wide catwalk at the top of the dam. From there she could reconnoiter. If she took the west stairway, there was the chance that she might get ahead of the creature, which would put him in the role of stalking her. She took the east stairs.

With the animal close by, Artemis was uneasy about keeping the crossbow uncocked in the duffel bag, but it wasn't possible to negotiate the steep stairway with the bag and the weapon cocked. She was winded as she negotiated the last few steps, thinking to herself that she'd been spending too much time in the lecture hall and not enough staying in shape. She crossed a small plaza lined with Roman-style columns and stepped out onto the top of the dam. As she put the bag down and loosened the straps to ready the arbalest, the clouds parted again and the dam was lit by brilliant moonlight. At the other end of the catwalk she saw the wolverine. He was running, with the loping gait of a small bear. Running toward her.

There was no escape except to try racing back down the precipitous stairway, and that would be a fool's last errand. She released the strap on her bag and drew the crossbow out. The strap wrapped around her left ankle, but she ignored it. There were scant seconds to load a bolt, set the trigger, and aim at the moving animal. She lifted the tiller into place against her shoulder, looked down the gun sight, and tried to estimate where the crosshairs would find the target after the few seconds it would take for her to pull the trigger and the arrow to travel. No time to calculate the speed or ballistics of the bolt, as she would have done in competition. This was life or death, fight with no chance of flight. The creature was halfway across the dam. She braced her back against the low retaining wall on the dry side of the twelve-story structure, nocked the bolt, and pulled the trigger. The light-weight bow recoiled further than her usual heavy vintage piece. She never saw where the bolt landed. The tiller leapt backward while her eye was still pressed against the gun sight, knocking her out cold. She collapsed on the retaining wall, halfway over the top edge. Only the weight of the spearhead in the duffel bag strapped to her ankle was preventing her from going over and dropping 130 feet. The strap began moving downward toward her toes, at which point she would be released into thin air.

Wulver reached her just as the strap came loose. His reflexes were like lightning. He dug a five-clawed paw into her left leg and pulled with the same force he could call up to hang on to a bull moose for hours before the larger animal was too exhausted to resist. He pulled Artemis off the wall, and she landed hard on the concrete catwalk.

CHAPTER 16

THE RESCUE

Artemis woke up. Her eyes adjusted slowly, gradually synching into stereo view as she came out of her fog. She was in an unfamiliar place. As she regained consciousness, she became aware of aching in her joints, a goose egg on her head, and a searing pain in her left calf. Someone spoke. She turned her head. A man with long white hair was standing across the room. He was stirring two cups of tea. He brought one to her. She sat up and sipped it.

"Who are you?"

"Alexander."

Wulver used the Greek root of Alistair.

"Last name?"

"Alexander is fine. And you are?"

"Artemis Fletcher. The last thing I remember, I was on an assignment near my house in Valhalla. Where am I now?"

"Not far from Valhalla. You had an accident. I was nearby. I brought you here."

"An accident. Why not the emergency room? The medical school is right down the road from there."

"That was not possible. I can't explain why at the moment. You were in danger. You are safe now."

"What kind of danger?"

Wulver hesitated.

"You had a fall, last night at the Kensico Dam. You were knocked unconscious."

"How did I get here?"

"I brought you here. It was the only possible place to go."

"So you rescued me after an accident, but you brought me here, wherever this is, instead of the hospital…"

"Miss Fletcher, there were…there are circumstances."

"I had a duffel bag and some, um, hardware."

"A weapon. I know. There wasn't time to retrieve those."

She looked around. Bookshelves lined the walls. The shadows were growing long. Soon the moon shining through the window would be the only light. Wulver spoke.

"Miss Fletcher. I'm sorry, but it's getting late, and you must leave quickly."

"Agreed, but where am I?"

Artemis was now recalling her mission, the trail to the dam, the steps. As the moonlight streamed through the leaded glass, she recalled the crossbow shot. She looked down at her left calf. Five long scratches were coated with some type of poultice, the medicine of a traditional culture.

"Alexander. The Scottish spelling for that is Alistair, correct?"

Wulver nodded slowly.

"You…you are…"

Wulver nodded again.

"I was sent to…"

"I know why you were sent. I know who sent you, and I know that you are required to report to the Strabo Society. Last night I could have…Moonlight is filling the room, Miss Fletcher. You must leave at once. We are in Scarborough. The country club is a quarter mile south on Route 9. Go now, please!"

Wulver walked her to the door.

"I see something in you that others saw in me. They saved me because I carry a certain power, an ancient power that must be preserved. That is why I brought you here and treated your wound. Now go. Walk south on Broadway to the country club, the old Woodlea Manor. You will get home safely from there. And please…"

"I know. Thank you."

He could feel it beginning again in the moonlight as she disappeared through the ivy-covered archway.

On Wednesday, December 14, Artemis Fletcher sent her report to Iverson by mail. It read:

Mission completed. North Westchester County wooded areas fully canvassed. No tracks or other evidence that would indicate presence in the county of the creature in question.

CHAPTER 17

YEAR'S END

Iverson was finalizing arrangements for the New Year's Day banquet. He would need to head straight to Macy's after work for Christmas gifts. The phone rang.

"Chuck, it's Chief Sean O'Malley, out here at Westchester police headquarters. Sorry to disturb you so close to the holidays. By the way, the wife and I are looking forward to January one!"

"Same here, Sean. What have you got for me?"

"Chuck, I think you should be aware of something a patrolman came across in Valhalla."

Iverson put the guest list down on his desk.

"Go on."

"I have a patrolman walk across the Kensico Dam every morning just after sunrise. A routine beat. Sometimes he finds an umbrella or a picnic basket left behind. On the morning of the fourth, he found a duffel bag with a clutch of some kind of arrows. The bow turned up later down at the bottom of the dam on the flats. Weird-looking thing. I sat on it until now because

I figured someone would come looking for it. I'm getting tired of looking at it, and to tell you the truth, it gives me the creeps. I went back through the bag yesterday, and I found something that's of interest to you, Chuck.

"What is it?"

"In the bottom of the bag is an envelope on Strabo Society stationery. That's why I picked up the phone to call you, Chuck."

"Did you open the envelope?"

"Nope. I'm a desk cop, Chuck, not a detective. It's your business."

"What else was in the bag?"

"Some sort of arrowhead. Big, hefty. There's one more thing, Chuck. There were muddy tracks on the catwalk. Led right up to the bag. Bigger than a German shepherd. Bear tracks, I would guess. None of it adds up to me."

"Sean, have you seen the arrowhead with your own eyes?"

"Sure I have, Chuck. Thought it might be evidence if a crime got reported."

"Tell me something, Sean. What color is it?"

"That's a bit weird as well. It's sort of white, or blue, maybe green. It keeps changing when you turn it around."

Bingo. Moonstone. It had to be from the Adirondacks. Iverson started connecting the dots on his legal pad. Wulver, wolverine tracks, Fletcher, crossbow, a moonstone spearhead. Fletcher must have tangled with Wulver. If she's still alive, she'll report back. In the meantime, that spearhead could be presented as Cardonas's discovery, which would clear his name and make him a hero. Then the artifact would go into the Strabo vault. That would keep Sinclair happy. The last piece of the puzzle would be to make sure Wulver was out of the picture.

"Hey, Chuck, you still on the line?"

"Sorry, Sean, just doing a little bit of thinking here. Since there's a Strabo letter in there, throw the whole pile of stuff in the duffel and have a plainclothesman drop it down here at the club. Maybe I can sort out the mystery."

"Will do. Merry Christmas, Chuck. See you at the banquet."

CHAPTER 18

THE BANQUET

January 1, 1961, New York City

The top floor of the Strabo Society clubhouse was generally used for viewing maps and photos, most of them kept in secrecy in the club's files. To this purpose, the ceiling was a large skylight to provide for maximum light in the capacious oak-lined chamber. It was opened once a year to nonmembers, specifically nonmembers who were inclined to make sizable donations to scientific societies. The attractions that drew them out of their Park Avenue suites on New Year's Day were the presentation of the Strabo Medal and the exotic dinner entrées from distant territories.

Iverson had been successful in keeping the entire Wulver situation under wraps. A scandal, especially one so bizarre, would have a negative impact on high-roller donations. As a matter of fact, he had a plan that might put the entire thing to bed once and for all. The first stage would play out at the banquet, and the second would require O'Malley's armed men out in Westchester.

As the plates were cleared and coffee was brought out, the guests filled out their silent auction cards and exchanged social register gossip. Iverson walked to the microphone and signaled for the cocktail pianist to fade out. He addressed the audience.

"Honored guests, we hope you have been edified, inspired, and most importantly well fed this evening."

Titters and a couple of "hear, hears" from the crowd.

"We now come to the main event, the presentation of the 1960 Strabo Society medal, the most distinguished award in the field of geography. Our ancient ancestor, Strabo, was the first honorary recipient. Although he lived far away and two millennia ago, as the first geographer he is certainly the progenitor of our field of endeavor.

"Now, before we present this year's award, we are honored to have in attendance my predecessor as society director, the distinguished Duncan Sinclair."

Applause.

"Dr. Sinclair is wearing the Strabo Medal of 1920 tonight."

More applause.

"In that year, he commissioned an expedition to the heart of the Adirondacks, to find hard evidence that would prove the presence of Iroquois hunters in the St. Regis wilderness, dating back much earlier than any known artifacts at the time. The expedition ended in tragedy. The leader did not return. His courage and determination to bring glory to the Society are an inspiration to all of us, and the exciting news I bring you tonight is that we have recovered the artifact he found before his tragic demise. It's an authentic Iroquois spearhead, of exceptional beauty, hand-knapped from hecatolite, a lustrous mineral found in the Adirondacks and thought by the tribes to have magical power drawn from the moon. As scientists, we can chuckle at the superstition, even as we stand in admiration of the beauty and historic significance of the piece, and the courage of the man who ventured into the wilderness to bring it back. Four decades on, we posthumously honor him tonight, with the first public viewing of his archaeological discovery, our recipient of the 1960 Strabo Medal, Dr. Anthony Cardonas!"

The audience erupted in applause, then a standing ovation as Iverson opened an oak box and held aloft the stone spearhead. He shouted over the continued applause.

"And receiving the medal for Dr. Cardonas is…"

He looked to his right into the wings and the blood ran out of his face.

"Wulver?"

The audience fell silent. Iverson was too shocked to move. He hadn't seen Wulver since they were both initiates in 1920, but it was unmistakably him. His hair was long and matted, his clothes spattered with mud. He stalked to centerstage, glancing warily at the audience. Iverson, in shock, still held the spearhead aloft. He stumbled backward as Wulver reached the podium. The ghostly apparition leaned toward the microphone and uttered two words.

"Cardonas…murdered…"

At that moment, the overcast winter sky over Manhattan parted, and the New Year's Day full moon flooded the hall with light. Wulver's eyes began to turn yellow, his teeth protruded in the image of a saber-toothed tiger, and his fur and claws burst through his bedraggled clothing. Before he dropped to all fours, he swatted the spearhead from Iverson's hands, seized it in his fangs, and leapt into the audience. Panic ensued as tables were overturned in a stampede of tuxedos and formal gowns. The beast raced down four flights of wide stairs, scattering socialites as he cut a swath past the front desk and out onto the marble steps leading to the street. The doorman overcame his shock at seeing a wild beast come crashing out of the club, and he began to blow his whistle in the hope that a nearby cop would radio for help.

Wulver looked around frantically as curious bystanders rushed toward him. He made it across the sidewalk to the edge of the street, and just as a police whistle blew around the corner on Fifth Avenue, a Willys Jeep roared up to the no-parking zone in front of the club entrance. Artemis was at the wheel. She gestured frantically to Wulver. He vaulted on powerful rear legs into the truck bed, and one minute later, they were six blocks uptown, heading toward the Henry Hudson Bridge and Scarborough thirty miles north.

CHAPTER 19

THE PANIC

The next two weeks were chaos. Iverson had, as usual, hired reporters and photographers to cover the award ceremony. Photos of the melee were on the front page of every daily paper. Typewriters across the city were frantically clicking in competition to come up with the most sensational headline. The *Herald Tribune* proclaimed WOLFMAN TERRORIZES A PARALYZED CITY, and the *Journal American* splashed THE BEAST THAT PURLOINED THE PRIZE over a photo of Wulver that planted the image of Iverson's terrified face in the mind of every New Yorker. The *Mirror*, the *Post*, and the *Daily News* went even further: NO ONE IS SAFE, THE GOTHAM GHOUL, and WHERE WILL HE STRIKE NEXT? The NYPD was getting a hundred calls a day reporting sightings of the creature in all five boroughs, and the police chief on Staten Island called for the formation of a *posse comitatis* to search block by block for the beast.

The intensity of the media frenzy threatened to overshadow the upcoming inaugural ceremony in Washington. On the CBS

Evening News, Huntley and Brinkley bantered back and forth about Hollywood coming to life. *Tonight Show* host Jack Paar quipped, "The NYPD is waiting for the monster to show his hand, er, paw." And on *Up to the Minute*, Walter Cronkite closed with the story, intoning, "Tonight, terror grips our largest and most populous city. And that's the way it is."

The worst part of the whole disaster, from Iverson's point of view, was that the great oak doors of the secretive Strabo Society had been thrown open on the front pages of every paper, and the news had gone national, all on his watch. He was not looking forward to hearing from Sinclair.

CHAPTER 20

ALBANY CALLING

Ewan ducked his head in the door of the study.

"Dr. Sinclair, excuse me, sir. The governor is on line one."

"Damn it. Put him through."

He picked up the receiver.

"Duncan, Nelson here. I was in Paris for New Year's, so I missed the banquet, but I understand that you put on quite a production this year. I'm assuming you've received and cashed the foundation's donation check?"

"Governor, the Society is eternally grateful for the family's support."

"Well, it may not be so eternal if you are somehow behind this werewolf business. Look, I'm trying to console Nixon, I've got Bob Moses pressuring me on his stadium project in Flushing, and now I've got a wolfman in Manhattan. Duncan, my people out at Kykuit are whispering that this critter is hiding out in Westchester. I've got a stone barn filled with cattle and sheep out there, and if this beast is the result of some crazy Strabo experiment, I'm going to hang you out to dry."

"For god's sake, Nelson, we don't create wolfmen over here. I sent this fellow on an expedition forty years ago. He vanished into thin air until two weeks ago. Iverson is still gulping Pepto-Bismol over it."

"Forget the excuses. I will put in a call to Chief O'Malley in Westchester and have his men comb the county. No furloughs until this animal is captured or killed. When I get down to Washington next week, I'll tell Bobby that the minute Jack is inaugurated, they need to throw everything they've got at this. Wall Street is on the brink of free fall. Who is your man at the club again?"

"Iverson. Chuck Iverson. A Yale man."

"I don't care if he's a graduate of Romper Room. Have him get on the stick and sort this out."

"Will do, governor. Thank you for the call."

The line went dead. Sinclair put down his receiver, took a long sip from his Glenlivet, then picked the phone up again and dialed Iverson's private line.

CHAPTER 21

THE HUNT

From January right through to the end of February, the switchboard at the *Tarrytown Daily News* was lit up with calls. A wolverine on the Tappan Zee Bridge; another one sniffing around the GM plant; monstrous apparitions prowling the Old Dutch Cemetery. Nothing panned out, of course, but the numerous references to the Tarrytown area lit a spark in the memory of a cub reporter.

Dido Parren typed the name *Wulver* on a blank sheet of onionskin. According to eyewitness accounts, that was the last word that Iverson had uttered before all hell broke loose at the Strabo banquet. She remembered that name from somewhere. It had something to do with her first days at the paper, back in October. When her shift ended, she asked her editor for permission to spend a couple of hours in the basement archive. She began the search with her first day at work, October 10. Parren combed meticulously through each page, scanning for the word *Wulver*. Nothing on the tenth. Nothing again on the eleventh, twelfth, or thirteenth. In the Thursday edition, dated October 14, she found the name. It was a letter to the editor, criticizing the paper for negative reporting about livestock found mysteriously killed in the area. The letter went on to defend carnivorous animals as acting on natural instinct.

It was signed, "Alistair Wulver, Graymalkin House, Scarborough."

Dido Parren knew she had her scoop. She had found the wolfman.

CHAPTER 22

THE GARDENER

Parren's front page byline was a short piece in the Wednesday edition under the headline IS THE WEREWOLF HIDING OUT IN SCARBOROUGH? She cited the letter to the editor and the anecdotal but strong clues that the author might himself be the creature who is half man, half wolverine. She ended with a request that anyone with information about a house with no street address, only the name Graymalkin, should contact the paper at once.

In the late afternoon, an elderly man appeared at the news desk. He said he had information for Dido Parren. The racket of her typewriter nearly drowned out his quiet voice. He had grown up in Ossining and left school in his teens to help support the family. He was working as a gravedigger in the Sparta Cemetery near the old Woodlea place when he was approached by a man named Van Leer. The upshot of it all, as he put it, was that he became the groundskeeper for Van Leer's estate, which Van Leer called Acheron. There was an extensive garden, including a collection of exotic willows. Spending so many of his days around the manor house and grounds, he became friendly with a boy whom he supposed to be Van Leer's son. They explored the riverbank and even canoed up to the rapids of the Croton River. He called his childhood friend Alex, but he remembered the old man calling him Alistair.

"So there was a large manor house on an estate. Were there any other buildings on the property?"

"Well, young lady, I haven't set foot there in forty years, but I hear that the big house is long gone. Bottom of the river, they say."

He sat silently with his eyes closed, visualizing.

"There was a gatehouse…behind a stone archway leading out to Route 9."

"Try to recall. Did that house have a name?"

"Van Leer was a bit of a strange duck. He had names for everything. He called the gatehouse Graymalkin."

Parren stood up and extended her right hand.

"Thank you, sir."

"I hope I've been of some help."

"You have."

Parren picked up the phone and dialed the US Geological Survey office in White Plains. She needed a map and, if possible, an aerial photo of the surroundings of the hamlet of Scarborough. She was put on hold while the clerk did some research. After being advised that any private Rockefeller property would be redacted, she was assured that the information she needed would come by courier before 9 p.m., including details of the country club, Revolutionary Road, Saint Mary's chapel, the Sparta Cemetery, and the ruins of the old Acheron Manor. And yes, it appeared from the photo that a gatehouse was indeed still standing, in a copse of what appeared to be willow trees.

Dido Parren asked the editor to hold the press and give her the lead story on page one.

CHAPTER 23

THE GATEHOUSE

Sinclair's phone rang early on Thursday. It was Iverson. Ewan put him right through.

"Damn it, Duncan. The cat is out of the bag. I'm heading out there right now."

By late afternoon of March 2, Iverson had taken charge of the operation. O'Malley had his men park dump trucks laterally across Route 9 at Sleepy Hollow bridge and five miles north at Ossining. Traffic was diverted up Bedford Road and through Briarcliff Manor. Scarborough was treated as a war zone.

That didn't stop dozens and eventually hundreds of river town residents, from Yonkers up to Peekskill, from converging on the area. Some were armed with shotguns, others with picks and axes. As the winter sky grew dark, the situation was volatile. The Westchester police were out in full force to hold back the crowd while they awaited orders from the chief.

The full moon rose, shining a bluish glow over the eerily calm scene within the barricades. O'Malley instructed his driver to slowly pull the squad car under the stone archway that bore the name *Acheron*. Iverson sat next to him in the back seat. They waited. There was no visible sign of life from the house. Uniformed cops set up brilliant floodlights aimed at the front of the building. Snipers armed with Ithaca 12-gauge shotguns crouched behind the eighteenth-century tombstones in the Sparta Cemetery, should the beast try to escape through a rear exit.

With the siege in place, O'Malley grew impatient. He rolled down his window and hoisted his bullhorn.

"Wulver, we know you are in there. Come out with your hands up!"

Iverson swatted the bullhorn from his hands.

"You nitwit! The moon is full. You're talking to a wolverine! What do you think this is, *High Noon*?"

At that moment, a sniper in the graveyard thought he spotted something moving by the old Model A. He opened fire, and at the sound, the dozen marksmen surrounding the building did the same. The rusty car was riddled with bullet holes, and soon the windows of the house were as well. O'Malley struggled to regain order, but the roar of the shotgun volley drowned him out. To the north, private citizens heard the gunfire. They surged forward, breaking through the line of officers assigned to hold them back. They advanced through the fields toward the cemetery.

Iverson, seeing that there was no way to get the bullets to return to the shotguns, told O'Malley to spread the order to advance on the house from all sides. They had to finish the job before every zealous citizen of the county converged on the scene. That would result in lethal chaos.

O'Malley gave the command, and he signaled for a Caterpillar bulldozer, parked next to the patrol car, to stand by, ready to advance. He raised his right hand, then brought it down like a checkered flag. The machine began rolling toward the front of the house. The instruction was to demolish the steps and continue straight through the front door, but after a few feet, the bulldozer ground to a halt. Something had flown out of the darkness from the willows above. With all lights trained on the house, no one could see the source. The first object was followed by another, and then another. The driver jumped off and ran toward the main road. When the hailstorm finally halted, Iverson left the patrol car and inspected the bulldozer. The vehicle's steel treads were immobilized, jammed with carbon arrows, each one pinpointed with deadly accuracy: crossbow bolts.

At that moment, with gunfire held, a great horned owl swept down from the stone archway. O'Malley and Iverson hit the deck as it swooped inches over their heads. They looked up to see it crash straight through the glass of a first-floor window without so much as slowing down. Now there were both an owl and a wolverine in the house, and a crossbow firing from the trees. Iverson knew this was not going well. He shouted at O'Malley to have his men continue advancing before the citizenry arrived en masse.

Inside the house, Wulver was crouched beneath the window that the owl shattered. Shards of glass rained down on him, but his fur was thick enough to withstand a rattlesnake bite. He shook it off. The owl perched on top of the grandfather clock, a Morbier from the 1850s that Van Leer had brought over long ago from France. The bird spoke in the voice of Deganawida.

"Wulver, I warned you about this day, and Van Leer came to you in the flames and did the same. These are the hills you wandered and the rivers you canoed, but there is no time to talk about that now. When I come down from this clock, put your full weight against it and push."

The owl vanished, and Deganawida appeared. He and Wulver pushed, the man with his shoulders and the wolverine with his massive front forepaws. The clock moved sideways, revealing two hinges in the floorboards. Deganawida lifted the trap door. The dirt floor underneath appeared to be solid.

The window to the right of the front door shattered, and a bottle wrapped in flaming rags came hurtling into the room. The dry, dusty carpet ignited.

"Dig, Wulver. Your five claws are the five nations. The generations dig with you. Put this in your jaw. Now use your claws and dig. Under that clay is Van Leer's tunnel. It opens on the bank of the great river."

He put the stone spearhead in Wulver's jaws.

"Now dig, my son, dig!"

The drapes were now on fire. Deganawida stood in the window, then ducked quickly as a hail of bullets burst through. He leapt on cat feet from window to window, drawing fire as Wulver dug.

After running a circuit that led the attackers to each of the first-floor windows, he arrived back at the front room. Wulver was gone. Deganawida closed the trap door and pushed the clock back in place. The fire was all around him. In a few minutes only the stone walls of the old house would be left standing.

With their eyes and guns trained on the doors and windows, none of the uniformed men noticed the owl fly out through the collapsed roof shingles, and no one saw the arbalist drop lightly from the branches of a willow tree. She vanished into the night as the flames gutted Graymalkin House.

In the morning, the Union Hose Company extinguished the last embers. Iverson picked through the wreckage. No sign of the target's remains, but no creature could have survived the inferno.

On Monday afternoon he telegraphed two words to Sinclair:

CASE CLOSED

PART TWO

The Arbalist

CHAPTER 24

THE MINESWEEPER

October 1963, Auvergne-Rhone-Alps, France

BLAM!

The explosion rocked Artemis Fletcher back on her heels. Even at fifty yards, the concussion was strong enough to knock her to the dirt, had she not known from long experience what to expect. Her Doc Marten boots were dug into the Alsace soil. She held her ground.

For two weeks she had been traveling up the Rhone valley from Marseilles, tracing the old route of a retreating Nazi division as they fled from Operation Dragoon, the second phase of D-Day. The invasion of the Riviera came weeks after the Normandy operation, when the better-equipped German forces were occupied trying to hold off the advancing Allies in the west. The straggling troops pursued by Dragoon in southern France left obstacles in the ground to slow the fury bearing down on them. They planted land mines—thousands, maybe millions, of them.

In their haste they kept no record of how many or where they were located. Two decades later Artemis, a champion crossbow competitor, was working with the French government's Department du Deminage to locate and safely explode the iron harvest, as the farmers called the lethal unexploded ordnance.

She ventured out from her hotel base at the Maison du Crible in Lyon at dawn each morning and traversed the A6 to the hazardous sites, including World War I battlefields in the Zone Rouge, regions still uninhabitable a half century after thousands of silently waiting World War I devices, some containing mustard gas, were buried. Arriving at a site, she would sit cross-legged and meditate for a full twenty minutes before venturing into the field. She needed to be totally calm and focused to work in regions designed to be deadly.

A decade earlier, Artemis was the world's foremost competitive crossbow archer. A historian by trade, she preferred to refer to herself using the old term: arbalist. Retired from the sport, she was teaching medieval history at Sarah Lawrence College in Bronxville, New York, but unknown to the students and faculty, she spent her time off traveling on missions for world governments, working with their most secretive agencies. After a chaotic job for the Strabo Society two years earlier, she had sworn off employment by private clients. Whispered enquiries seeking crossbow experts typically had an air of criminality, and Artemis was no assassin. In fact, she was spending her evenings off in France studying the medieval honeycomb of alleys and passageways in the old quarter, Vieux Lyon, as part of her scholarly studies.

After a day firing explosive draglines across minefields up near the Vosges Mountains and the five-hour drive back to Lyon, Artemis was glad to get back to the Maison du Crible, where she could relax and have a glass of wine in the *bouchon*. She was savoring a duck confit with a side of dandelion salad when the hotel manager came over.

"*Excusez-moi,* madam. There is a telegram for you at the front desk, marked urgent."

It was from Reston Grocery Distribution, which Artemis understood was CIA headquarters in Langley, Virginia.

```
URGENT. EYES ONLY. MEET DRIVER HOTEL LOBBY
5 AM FOR TRANSPORTATION TO ORLY AIRPORT.
BOOKED AIR INDIA TO NEW DELHI ETD 10 AM,
WEST TERMINAL. DIPLOMATIC PROTOCOL: SPECIAL
GEAR OK. ON ARRIVAL NEW DELHI PROCEED TO
MAIDENS HOTEL. AWAIT FURTHER.
```

Apparently the mission in France was over. Artemis packed her medieval history notes, then broke down her travel crossbow and secured it in her duffel bag. Her diplomatic credentials would enable her to travel to India with the weapon in an overhead compartment. She was going to miss Lyon, so she decided to take one last walk along the cobblestones of the old quarter. With her trained eye, she had spent her September evenings discovering the hidden entrances to the network of passageways that had served as a means of surreptitious travel from the Middle Ages right through to the Resistance movement in World War II. As a historian, she reveled in the lore of it all.

There was a sidewalk cafe where customers who desired to use the *toilette* could duck their heads and pass through a fourteenth-century archway, then descend a stone staircase through an ancient oak door, and finally turn left into the restroom area. Artemis's curiosity had led her, weeks earlier, to turn *a droite* instead of *a gauche*, down a dark hallway that required a flashlight, something restaurant patrons didn't carry but of course Artemis did. Another heavy oak door opened out into an enclosed courtyard, and from that point the secret alleys of Lyon were unveiled to her.

On her last night in the city, she quietly pushed open the old door, turned on her headlamp, closed the door, and then put a strip of white tape from the thumb turn over onto the doorjamb.

She prowled the dark alleys, making a circuit around the Place Neuve Saint-Jean without seeing another person or being seen. She stopped at one point when she thought she heard the sound of footsteps behind her. She wrote it off as an overactive imagination in a spooky place. At the end of the circuit she was back at the oak door. The tape was broken. Someone had followed her. Her weapon was packed away, back at the hotel.

Unarmed and assigned to an early-morning CIA mission, Artemis was not looking for a confrontation. It was probably a curious tourist, maybe another history professor. She returned to the hotel to get a few hours of sleep. As she walked through the courtyard to her room, she glanced up at la Tour Rose, the pink tower that was the hotel's landmark. A man was looking directly down at her from a fourth-floor window. He was tall, with a shock of red hair. Artemis chuckled, talking softly to herself.

"Well, if he's following me, he's not a real counterspy. Way too easy to recognize, and if he is, I hope he's prepared to go halfway around the world first thing in the morning!"

Artemis walked up to her *chambre* and double-locked the door.

CHAPTER 25

IVERSON'S PROBLEM

Two weeks earlier, Strabo Society headquarters, New York City

Iverson was jotting down notes on a yellow legal pad. His conversation with Sinclair had been brief but concise. There had been no time for congratulations on the elimination of the monster. The Society had to be buttoned up again. Too much was thrown open to the city, to the world. Public curiosity would lead to scrutiny, and that's the last thing the club wanted. Sinclair was clear about that.

There was something else bothering Iverson about the Scarborough incident. He had voiced his concern to Sinclair on the phone.

"Duncan, time has gone by, things have settled down a bit over the past couple of years, but there's a detail that's been bothering me."

"Wulver was located, the house was destroyed, with him in it. So what's bothering you?"

"That big D9 bulldozer that we brought in to ram down the front door."

Sinclair snorted.

"The damn thing stalled out, if I recall correctly. Waste of money."

"It didn't stall out, Duncan. It was knocked out of commission. I was right there. It advanced a few feet, came to a dead stop. The driver jumped ship and made tracks off the property."

"I can hardly blame him, given the melee, but go on."

"The treads were clogged. We had to have it towed out in the morning. Ever try to tow a twenty-nine-ton bulldozer?"

"The treads were clogged with what?"

"Arrows. Crossbow arrows."

Sinclair stirred the ice in his whiskey glass and sighed.

"You're telling me it was Artemis Fletcher."

"She's the only crossbow archer that comes to mind who might be taking potshots at our bulldozer, Duncan."

"Wasn't she in our employ?"

"She reported to me by mail that she'd canvassed Westchester and found no sign of Wulver. That's the last we heard from her."

"Damn it, Chuck. Her old man and I fought side by side in France in the Fourteenth Brooklyn, the Park Slope Armory boys. He was a hell of an archer himself. Well, where is she now?"

"I contacted Sarah Lawrence. She's on sabbatical for the entire year. No forwarding address."

Long pause.

"Chuck, I recommended her, and if she double-crossed the Society, I take full responsibility for that. But we need to move forward on two fronts, and I want you to make the next hire, someone outside of my circle. Find a young man like the unfortunate fellow who ran up against Wulver…"

"Macduff."

"Like Macduff. Someone untethered, with a background in espionage. We need to find Fletcher, and we need to check off the boxes on the Society acquisition list. I'm eighty years young, Chuck, and I need to know that my legacy is in place, and by that I mean in the third-floor vault at the club."

"Both of those jobs are going to need someone discreet."

"Correct. I'm out here in the Hamptons, where no one is discreet. Contact Fordham, Chuck, and hire a man who can go undercover. Supply him with whatever portfolio of passport identities he will need, and send him out there. Now, if you will excuse me, I have a date with a bottle of Glenlivet."

Sinclair hung up.

CHAPTER 26

DOYLE'S INTERVIEW

The front desk clerk directed Tom Doyle to the library. Iverson waved the younger man over to his table.

"Doyle. Iverson here. Call me Chuck. Sit down."

Iverson lit his pipe and shook the match out.

"First off, whatever is said at this table stays strictly between us. Understood?"

"Understood."

"You're a Fordham grad, correct?"

"Class of 1960. Law enforcement with a specialty in espionage. Then two years as a Navy frogman, underwater demolition team."

"Did you know Kevin Macduff?"

"At Fordham, yes, but I knew him before that. We were both at Bronx Latin. He grew up in Woodside, Queens. I grew up in South Boston. We had a lot in common, not just the red hair. Good man."

"He was in our employ for a short time. I'm looking for someone who can carry out a few jobs for the Strabo Society. We avoid any and all publicity. You would be traveling around the globe, reporting back directly to me and no one else. Understood?"

"Understood."

"I'm going to give you a general overview. After that you will only receive specific instructions to follow to the letter, but you will be in situations where you will need to think on your feet."

Doyle nodded slowly, keeping his eyes fixed on Iverson's.

"Here's the overview. We need to find a woman who has vanished, leaving a bit of unfinished business with the club. An associate of ours at the Université de Lyon thinks she may be there. You will need to leave for France within the next week."

"Got it. What do I do when I locate her?"

"Report back to me. I will tell you how to proceed. However, she is to be considered armed and dangerous. Whatever decisions you have to make on the spot, the club will cover for you."

Iverson cleared his throat.

"There is another bit of overseas business that I need you to handle. Do you know the name Duncan Sinclair?"

"I made some inquiries. He's one of the Society's founders, correct?"

"Correct. Since the 1920s, he has been amassing a collection. Fossils, cultural artifacts, the kind of things you might expect in a geography society's vault. Over the past two decades, since his official retirement as director, he's expanded the program to include works of art. Priceless works. Cornerstones of the history of nations."

"And if those cornerstones belong to the nations, how does he go about acquiring them?"

"Any way he can. That's where you come in. This isn't the Met, Doyle. We don't put things on display for the public. Once these pieces go into our vault up on the third floor, they never again see the light of day, but the club becomes wealthier than…"

Iverson cut himself off.

"You don't need to know the ethics or the importance of Sinclair's legacy. We just need you to follow instructions and take initiative when you are on your own on the far side of the globe."

Iverson puffed on his pipe.

"I'm not going to ask if you have any questions, because I'm not going to answer any questions. I've told you everything you need to know. Go where we send you, and find the girl with the crossbow. Also, try not to wind up MIA."

"Like Macduff?"

"Like I said, no more questions. You're hired, Doyle. Check in to the Savoy and await further instructions."

The two men rose and shook hands.

CHAPTER 27

THE LIBRARIAN

Alexander Wolfe squinted through his glasses at the young woman's library card.

"Dido Parren. What a fascinating name! Do you know that Dido was in love with the Trojan Aeneas, and when a jealous goddess fooled her into thinking that he had dumped her, she—"

"Immolated herself on a flaming pyre."

Parren smiled as she finished his sentence.

"My, my, young lady. You know your classical literature. You might consider joining our Fable and Fairy Tale Club here at the library. We meet once a month."

"I'd love to, Mister…"

"Wolfe. Alexander Wolfe. Everyone here just calls me Alex."

"Well, I'd love to, Alex, but I got a promotion at work last year, and I don't have much time to read books. I'm always reading newsprint."

"Newsprint! And what is the new job?"

"I'm editor of the Sunday edition of the *Tarrytown Daily*

News. I only started at the paper not quite three years ago, but after I broke the story on the werewolf, I went straight to the front of the line for the editor's job when he retired."

"The werewolf story! So that was you. You should be very proud. I imagine you are somewhat of a celebrity now in our little river town."

"Not really. I'm too busy for that, but I do get stopped on the street by people who thank me. They feel safer with that creature gone."

"And well they should. I see it's almost seven. Anything else I can help you with?"

"No, thanks. Enjoy the evening. I love the big full moon in October, don't you?"

"Oh yes, I do indeed. The hunter's moon, they call it."

He removed the card from the back of her book and placed it in the "out" index drawer.

"You're all checked out. Nice meeting you, Miss Parren."

CHAPTER 28

THE HUNTER'S MOON

Alex Wolfe checked the stacks and knocked on the restroom doors to make sure that the Warner Library was empty. Then he turned out the lights, set the thermostat at sixty degrees, locked the heavy iron front door, and then locked the side door behind him. The October air was cool. That was good. He had several miles to travel. Instead of turning down Broadway toward town as he usually did, he walked briskly straight up McKeel Avenue. At the top of the hill, he crossed onto the Marymount campus. On the far side of the convent, he found the old Putnam Railway trail. He followed it to the edge of the Rockefeller estate and then turned downhill on County House Road. He had traveled this way many times as a boy, to visit the two small Tarrytown Lakes that supplied the town's water.

There was once a small village, Eastview, on the east end of the lakes. It was there when he left as a young man on the expedition to Floodwood, but it was gone when he returned from the north woods forty years later. He remembered the almshouse where the homeless lived. Abandoned children, babies left on doorsteps, lived there as well. Most spent their lives at the alms-house, and when they died, they were buried in a cemetery right on the property. When the railroad was moved from up the hill to down by the Sawmill River, the entire town was razed. Every month, as he passed the site, he could hear the voices of the children buried beneath the roadbed. Having lost his own brother-hood with the living, he found kinship with the dead.

Wulver lay on the tracks. He listened to the little ones crying, and he heard the worried voices of the old ones. He talked with them, told them to take heart that they'd been given a proper burial, and even another burial over that one, while he'd been left for dead at the bottom of a lake far from home. He told them how much he loved the hills of the county, and how lucky they were to sleep forever in those hills. He would never sleep. As he lay on the hill and talked, the hunter's moon rose. Wulver's claws grew longer. They began to dig into the clay. His fur grew thick and his voice became a rasping growl. He had to keep moving.

He waded the shallow Sawmill River and continued uphill and across the Valhalla cemetery, where he heard more voices, but he couldn't stop to listen. He skirted around the village of Valhalla and bounded on all fours up the long steps to safety at the top of the Kensico Dam. He heard more voices, from the drowned town at the bottom of the reservoir, and from the tribes who lived in the valley long before, when it was Otter Path. He also heard the voices of the men who fell during the construction of the dam, men still entombed deep in the quick-drying concrete. Wulver rested and listened. He felt pity for them, and he recalled how he felt pity for the woman he found injured on the dam three years before. That was the first time that Wulver, the beast, felt the emotion of Wulver, the man. Compassion, pity. He rescued the woman instead of following his wolverine instinct, and ever since that night he came to the dam on the full moon, meditating on compassion and pity. After a few minutes he padded across the catwalk and continued on the trail to Cranberry Lake. There he made his way deep into the old quarry, where he would sequester himself for three days and nights while the moon was full.

As far as Dido Parren and the other residents of Westchester were concerned, the beast had died when Graymalkin House burned. Only Alexander Wolfe, the Tarrytown librarian, knew the truth: that Alistair Wulver had actually died long before on Floodwood Pond, but he was very much present in their midst.

CHAPTER 29

THE BOOK MARKET

Artemis Fletcher slept for most of the trip to India, waking briefly at a fueling stopover in Tehran. She flashed her diplomatic credentials in New Delhi and was waved through immigration. Cabs waited outside the terminal to ferry Western tourists and businesspeople to the hotels. The check-in clerk at Maidens Hotel looked at her passport, then disappeared into the back office. She came out with a sealed diplomatic pouch. Artemis carried her own duffel bag along with the pouch up to her room. She was sleepy, but she read the instructions and set the alarm clock before turning in.

2 PM Daryaganj Book Mart. Metro to Delhi Gate station. Look for Ganesh bookstall with elephant flag. Ask for Birindar.

Good. An afternoon meeting would give her a little time to get over the time zone change. She hung the do not disturb sign on her door.

Artemis woke at noon and found the metro station. She disembarked at Delhi Gate and walked into a world of books. The instructions were to find the Ganesh stall, but she indulged in a bit of shopping along the way, finding Macaulay's 1871 *History of England* in a lovely three-volume edition; not something one could take globetrotting, sadly. Then she spotted the elephant flag.

"Good afternoon."

The clerk had a beard and full mustache, and he wore Sikh attire, with a turban, and had a long dagger hanging from the belt of his tunic. He spoke perfect Queen's English.

"Good afternoon, miss. Lovely day."

"I'm looking for Birindar. Is he here today?"

"Of course, miss. He is expecting you."

The clerk pointed to a younger man, also Sikh. He was straightening rows of used medical textbooks, all in English.

"Good afternoon, Birindar."

"Good afternoon, madam. Lovely to see you. I have a gift for you from a Mr. Langley."

He handed Artemis a paperbound book, *Voice of the Himalayas* by Swami Sivananda.

"Much wisdom in this book, madam, especially on page one forty-two."

Artemis started to open the book. Birindar, suddenly serious, put his hand quickly over the cover. He looked to the right and the left, and waited until a browsing tourist moved on. He lowered his voice.

"Return to the Maidens Hotel. Go to your room and lock the door. Listen for footsteps in the hallway. When all is quiet, open to page one forty-two, but not before then. Understood?"

"Yes."

He raised his voice in a jovial way.

"Then all is good! I wish you the best on your travels. I send you a blessing for your safety; God is love, love is God. Good luck and I hope to see you again."

Artemis enclosed the book under her jacket and made her way through the growing throng of book browsers. It was getting hot, and the crowd was merging into a mélange of colorful costumes. As she passed through the front gate, she thought she caught a glimpse of a shock of red hair, but it disappeared into the sea of Sunday market-goers. She returned to the hotel, took all the precautions, and opened the book to page 142. There she found three train tickets, a bus ticket, a hotel reservation, and a typed itinerary.

Yellow line Metro to New Delhi Railway Station. Satyagrah Express dest. Raxaul. ETD 7 AM. Two rail connections. Bus across border via Tribhuvan Highway to Kathmandu. Check in Dwarika's Hotel. Await contact: Norbu

So the agency was sending her onward to Nepal, and thence maybe into the Himalayas. This was getting more interesting all the time…

A mile away at the Western Union office, Tom Doyle wired a message to Iverson in New York.

```
TARGET LOCKED. UNDER SURVEILLANCE. ALSO
HIMALAYAN THANGKA CACHE STRONG LEAD.
WILL UPDATE.
```

CHAPTER 30

NORBU

The six-hundred-mile train journey to the Nepalese border gave Artemis a chance to page through the *Voice of the Himalayas* book in which Birindar had tucked her tickets. On a secret mission to a land rarely visited by outsiders, especially Westerners, she was eager to pick up any and all words of wisdom. It was a book of encouraging aphorisms.

> *Attune yourself to the infinite by stilling the mind.*
> *Understand well the meaning of life and then start the quest.*
> *Be bold. Be brave. Dare. Be up and doing!*
> *Waste not a second.*

Artemis committed a few of Sivananda's phrases to memory. She had a feeling she might be needing them.

At Raxaul, she boarded a third train that would take her across the border into Nepal. Once in the country, she could access the Tribhuvan Highway bus route to the outskirts of Kathmandu. There she would finally secure transportation into the isolated

city. Kathmandu was protected by the natural massif of the Siva-
lik Hills. The highway through the region was an unending series
of white-knuckle switchbacks with breathtaking views, including
Mount Everest, the highest point on the planet, to the east.

After a long day of overland travel across the subcontinent,
Artemis disembarked at Durbar Square and hailed a taxi to
Dwarika's Hotel. She was approached in the hotel lobby by a
young woman dressed in a modern version of *kurta* style: knit
trousers covered by a knee-length wool tunic and a bright red silk
scarf. She had long, glossy black hair, almond-shaped green eyes,
and polished olive skin.

"You are a friend of Mr. Langley?"

Artemis nodded. The woman smiled and extended her right hand.

"Norbu Miller."

"Artemis Fletcher. Pleased to meet you."

"Call me Norbu. It means jewel. We have a traditional image
here of the jewel in the lotus, meaning the spirit that resides
within. You will find that kind of imagery everywhere in the
Nepalese culture. Of course, Miller is not a common surname
here! My husband and I met in advanced history studies at Harvard three years ago. We both teach at Golden Gate College,
right down the road from the hotel."

Artemis was relieved to meet up with a history professor, a
kindred spirit, there at the remote rooftop of the world. The two
women sat in the lobby and chatted, sipping sweet tea with milk.

"I imagine you need a day to rest up and adjust to the eleva-
tion. We are in the foothills of the highest peaks in the world.
Spend tomorrow afternoon in the spa. I will return at four p.m.,
and then we can talk about various matters."

Norbu excused herself and Artemis checked in at the front
desk, making an appointment for a steam bath and massage in
the morning.

CHAPTER 31

DURBAR SQUARE

Artemis signed in at the spa at 10 a.m. The receptionist glanced at her name, and then called to her manager. The two women spoke briefly in Nepali, then the manager produced two gym bags.

"These were left for you, Miss Fletcher."

In the locker room, Artemis opened the bags. The first contained a full *kurta suruwal* outfit, which she hung in her locker. The second bag contained head-to-toe L.L.Bean hiking clothes and a pair of Alpine climbing boots.

After her spa treatments, she donned the *kurta* and went down to the lobby to meet Norbu.

"Can I call you Artemis? Let's skip the hotel dining room. You want to sample some Nepalese street food while you are here in the city."

A food truck was parked alongside the Golden Gate campus, serving basic meals to students and faculty between classes. The two women dined on *dal bhat*, the staple rice and lentil soup, and *momo* dumplings.

"Now we will do a bit of tourism. It's not like Times Square here, or even Harvard Square. Kathmandu is a destination for pilgrims, and every aspect of life is spiritual. Let's take a little stroll."

They taxied to the hustle and bustle of Durbar Square, and then walked down a side street thronged with pilgrims.

"Is this a shrine?"

"Indeed, but it's a different kind of shrine. This one is to a living goddess, Taleju. This is her palace, the Kumari Ghar."

"The goddess lives in this palace?"

"Yes. Through infinite incarnations, the goddess lives forever. She incarnates in the physical presence of a young girl. When that girl becomes a woman, Taleju reincarnates in a new young girl. That girl is called the Kumari Devi, the living goddess. These pilgrims come from all over to get a glimpse of her."

Artemis's friendship with Alistair Wulver, back in Westchester, made her one of the few Westerners who had had a firsthand encounter with the reanimation of a soul. She said nothing about that to Norbu, however, continuing to keep her vow of silence to Wulver.

"Artemis, I brought you here for a reason."

"And that is?"

"The goddess has requested your presence."

CHAPTER 32

KUMARI DEVI

A trained spy, Artemis was expert at concealing emotion, but she couldn't help raising an eyebrow. Norbu, also schooled in spy craft, noticed her surprise and turned the conversation to logistics.

"Security is very tight at the palace, but you have been cleared for all access. Artemis, the goddess has requested to see you alone. I will wait for you outside of her chambers."

The palace guards recognized their credentials and ushered them inside. Norbu waited in an opulent anteroom while Artemis was led to the door of Kumari's chamber. Her escort opened the door, bowing deeply, and then vanished. Artemis entered the room.

It was dark. Aloeswood incense permeated the air. The throne was an overstuffed cushion covered in silk. A girl who looked to be around ten years old was seated on it. She was wrapped in a metallic gold sari, with a triangular crimson silk crown covering her forehead. There was no one else in the room. The young girl was chanting softly, *"Om mani padme hum,"* the same mantra that

Artemis chanted before walking onto a minefield. She joined in, whispering.

After several minutes, Kumari Devi opened her eyes, acknowledging Artemis's presence. The dim light, the incense, the silk hangings all contributed to a state of deep meditation. Artemis felt that she was floating on a still pond, absent of any need for volition or action. Her eyelids were heavy, but she was not sleepy. She felt a heightened awareness. As she looked at Kumari, the young girl underwent a visual transformation. She seemed to melt or dissolve into particles that hung like jewels in the incense-laden air. The jewels rearranged themselves into a bird, a goose that perched regally on the throne. As Artemis looked, as if through a veil, the goose transmogrified into a woman. She wore a deerskin tunic and a necklace of shells. Her face was decorated with Iroquois war paint, red on one side, blue on the other. She spoke, in English.

"Artemis. I am Sky Woman, the creator. My palace is in the high peaks of the Adirondacks, far from here, but I am in no way constrained there. The peaks here, the highest of all, are my home as well. I am worshiped here as Hamsa, the mother goddess, and I am the only bird who can fly above Chomolungma, the place that you call Everest."

Artemis listened as if in a dream.

"I appear as a young girl, as a golden eagle or a goose, in any form I choose. I called you here because you are in danger. You are being hunted. You have a mission in the high peaks, but you will be troubled by your hunters. I know you well, because you helped my son, Deganawida, to save his own son, Wulver. You are the only one living who knows Wulver's secret, and so I protect you. Tomorrow you will go up into the mountains. When you need more strength than your fragile human body holds, call on me, Hamsa."

Artemis, in a hypnotic state, whispered the name.

"Hamsa."

Sky Woman dissolved into the incense smoke. The young Kumari sat once again on her cushion, eyes closed, still chanting.

"Om mani padme hum."

The door behind Artemis opened, and she left the room. She and Norbu walked silently back into Durbar Square and took a taxi back to the hotel. Norbu advised her to get some sleep.

"We meet here at six a.m. I will be driving a Land Rover. Leave the *kurta* here and wear the trekking gear. And Artemis— bring your crossbow."

CHAPTER 33

THE LETTER

At 5:30 a.m., Artemis jotted down a note on hotel stationery.

Alistair,

Up into Himalayas today. May not survive. Sky Woman present but future unknown. Hope to see you again in some way, someday.

Artemis

She tucked the letter into an envelope and addressed it to *A. Wolfe, Warner Library, Tarrytown, N.Y., U.S.A.*

It was against mission policy to use the regular mails, but this couldn't go through Agency channels. She left it with the night desk clerk for afternoon pickup.

Artemis sat in the lobby and sipped a cup of tea while she waited for Norbu. She thanked the night desk clerk when the shift changed, and they exchanged good luck wishes.

The Land Rover pulled up at six on the dot, and Artemis climbed in, placing her duffel bag carefully behind her seat. The sun was coming up as they headed northeast out of town, toward the Himalayan massif.

At 7 a.m., a tall, red-haired man approached the front desk. He greeted the morning clerk warmly.

"Subha prabhata!!"

"And good morning to you as well, sir."

"I believe a guest, Fletcher is the name, left an envelope for me. Address is in the USA."

The clerk shuffled through the papers left by the departed night clerk.

"Fletcher, Fletcher. Ah yes, here it is. Tarrytown, New York?"

"Yes, that's it. Splendid."

She handed him the envelope. Doyle placed it in his backpack.

"Have a wonderful day, Mr. Wolfe."

"Oh, I will. I will."

CHAPTER 34

CHO OYU

Alone together in the Land Rover, Artemis and Norbu could finally speak freely.

"Artemis, do you know the nature of your mission?"

"I knew to meet you at the hotel in Kathmandu. That's it."

"This is a dangerous assignment. I'm sure you know that India and China waged a one-month territorial war up in the highlands just a year ago. The border is still unclear, and Chinese troops could be patrolling anywhere."

"So it's not Yeti I'm watching out for?"

"Artemis, I have seen reports about the werewolf in your home country three years ago, so perhaps you have your own version of Yeti. No, it's not Yeti or Chinese soldiers that worry me up here. It's mercenaries."

"Hired guns…What are they doing in the Himalayas?"

"Let me give you a bit of backstory. Have you ever heard the name Duncan Sinclair?"

This time, Artemis stayed in control, showing no emotion.

"I know the name. A founder of that geographic group, the Strabo Society."

"To the academic community, they are known as a scientific think tank, but to the Agency, they are at the top of our list of international thieves. Sinclair is elderly, and he's become increasingly obsessed with amassing the world's greatest cultural treasures before he dies. The problem is, those treasures are not for sale, and he will stop at nothing to get them."

Norbu glanced at Artemis, then fixed her eyes back on the narrow highway. They were climbing above ten thousand feet, and she had to keep her mind alert in the sparse oxygen.

"Artemis, your name has come up in intercepted communications. Strabo has hired an agent to find you. He has permission to deal with you in any way he sees fit. Apparently they link you to the werewolf incident that caused them a lot of embarrassment a couple of years ago. If they see you standing in their way, they will be looking to eliminate you. The intercepted communique suggests that they know you are in Kathmandu."

"So there is a target on my back, but Norbu, you still haven't told me what my mission is."

"Four years ago, the Chinese took control of Lhasa, the capital of Tibet. The Dalai Lama was held under virtual house arrest. Because of his charismatic power over the Tibetan population, it was inevitable that he would be imprisoned or worse. I can't tell you how I know this, but I will tell you that there are agents in Langley who can relay the story firsthand. The Dalai Lama was disguised as a soldier and walked out of his palace undetected. He came across the Himalayas on horseback, and as you may know, he is safe and well, at least for the moment, down in India."

"I know the parts of that story that have come out in the American papers. So what does it have to do with us driving into the mountain range?"

"He was accompanied on his trek by a number of monks, all marked like him for execution back in Tibet. They brought with them what treasures they could carry from the Potala, the royal palace. They were clerics, spiritual people, so gold was unimportant to them. The priceless treasure they loaded on pack animals was a collection of the oldest and most sacred *thangka* paintings. They were rolled and carried in metal tubes. Some were reputed to date back to the beginnings of Tibetan Buddhism, the coming of Ashoka in the third century BC. To make a long story short, the Strabo Society wants those paintings."

"Where are they?"

"Midway through the escape, it was decided that the trove of paintings and the Dalai Lama should be traveling separately, so that in a worst case they wouldn't both be apprehended in a single stroke. Four monks left the party on foot with two yaks bearing the treasure. They headed up the nineteen-thousand-foot Nangpa La pass crossing the Himalayas, and simply disappeared, along with the treasure."

"Disappeared until…?"

"Until recently when Sherpas came down from Cho Oyu, one of the peaks near Everest. The summit is the sixth highest point on our planet. The name means 'turquoise goddess.' It is a holy mountain, with a few flat plateaus on the northwest face. Last year, Sherpas found the frozen remains of four monks at the mouth of a rocky cave enclosed in a massive ice cliff at twenty-one thousand feet. There was no sign of the treasure, but it's thought that the tubes either went down a crevasse, or they are hidden deep in that cave. Your mission is to find the *thangka*s and arrange for their safe delivery to the Dalai Lama in Dharamshala. To do that, you'll need to survive both the mountain itself and Sinclair's men, who may already be there ahead of you."

So Duncan Sinclair, her father's old friend, was sending

agents halfway around the world to kill her because she stood in the way of his stealing sacred icons of Buddhism. Artemis was silent for a while as they climbed higher.

"We will stay in the village of Tingri for a few days, getting used to the fourteen-thousand-foot altitude. That's the easy part. Then we'll trek up to base camp at sixteen thousand feet. From there, it's a rocky day climb up a field of glacial scree to the plateau bordered by ice cliffs at twenty-one-thousand feet. That's where we hope to find the paintings."

CHAPTER 35

THE DOYLE COMMUNIQUE

Tom Doyle stashed the letter unopened in his pack. There would be time to read it and write a full report after the business of the next few days. He dashed off a quick telegram to Iverson.

```
HEADING TO CHO OYU SITE. TARGET ALSO EN
ROUTE. EXPECTING CONFRONTATION AND GOOD
OUTCOME. HAVE PASSWORD TO GAIN ACCESS TO
HAWKER PROTOTYPE VERTICAL TAKEOFF CRAFT.
LOOKING FORWARD TO PLAYING WITH THAT TOY.
EXPECT OUT OF TOUCH FOR THREE DAYS.
```

He headed straight to an unmarked hangar at the small Kathmandu airport.

CHAPTER 36

THE TREK

Norbu trained Artemis in the basics of Himalayan mountaineering. The hazard factor was a combination of rugged terrain, lack of oxygen, and deep crevasses covered with a thin layer of ice and snow, making them hard to detect. That trifecta combined with the ever-present avalanche threat and, in this case, ruthless thieves competing for the same prize made this a perfect storm of danger. Norbu made that clear as she unfolded the map and outlined the trail up Cho Oyu.

"Even though we're not attempting to summit, and the weather is on our side, there's still no shortage of ways to die up there."

At first light they started up the long dirt track that led to the preset orange base camp tents, the starting point up the northwest ridge trail. Artemis and Norbu were accompanied by three Sherpas, one of whom, Babu, knew the location of the supposed *thangka* treasure cave. At base camp, the Sherpas would wrangle two draft yaks on which they hoped to load the priceless paintings. Norbu reminded Artemis once again that the high zone was not a place to linger. Low oxygen made judgment cloudy, and experienced climbers had made bad, sometimes fatal, decisions up on the peaks. Even the intermediate plateaus were subject to avalanches roaring down from the immense snow mass that covered the upper reaches of the peak. The party was hoping to ascend to twenty-one thousand feet, locate the paintings, and quickly bring them back down to Tingri and from there to the Golden Gate campus, where they could be kept securely before transfer down to India. They all knew it couldn't be that simple.

They rested overnight at base camp, and then continued before daylight upward toward the high plateau where they hoped the cave held the treasure. Most of the climb was free of fresh snow, but the trek over an endless field of glacial rocks made every step an exercise in extreme care and control. The effort was offset by the spectacular deep blue sky, the towering rock and ice formations, and the sight, at every glance to the southeast, of Mount Everest, the highest point on Earth. At twenty thousand feet, they came to a rope bridge, with two cables supporting a plank deck. Two ropes for hand grips were stretched above the main cables. Babu stepped lightly onto the deck. He changed his gait, gliding smoothly across the planks. Norbu whispered to Artemis.

"You have to walk differently across a rope bridge. If you put your full weight down, each new step will require you to reposition yourself, almost like climbing. Watch Babu. The Sherpa people invented the rope bridge centuries ago."

Babu returned and stepped once again onto the bridge, this time leading one of the yaks. Artemis marveled at his nonchalant courage in risking his life to ensure the safety of the party. Halfway across, he motioned for the rest to cross, one at a time. Norbu went first, with Artemis watching her technique. Artemis went next, followed by the two Sherpas leading the remaining yak.

Once safely across, they kept moving. They needed to use every minute of daylight to get back down to base camp before dark.

They reached the rocky plateau, walled by an edifice of ice and rock as tall as a fifteen-story building, at noon. Babu spoke quietly to Norbu, who conveyed the message to Artemis.

"This is where the monks were found. They have undergone the Buddhist rite of passage and are no longer here. The cave is in that cliff face."

Artemis had been hearing a quiet but consistent buzzing sound in her ears for an hour. She attributed it to the odd symptoms of oxygen deprivation, but as it grew louder, she could only guess that it was the whir of helicopter blades, even though logic told her it was impossible for a helicopter to reach the altitude of the plateau. She blinked in surprise when a strange aircraft appeared, banking down over the ice wall and slowing down as if to make a vertical landing. She shouted to Norbu.

"Tell Babu to get his men in the cave!"

The tiny craft buzzing directly over the plateau wasn't like any helicopter Artemis had ever seen. Four vertical jets mounted on the undercarriage were blasting downward, but the sound they produced was too quiet to be generated by any stock jet engine. This was something altogether different. The vertical jets kept the craft hovering like a hummingbird. Fascination trumped caution as Artemis couldn't resist a visual check of what must have been a top-secret prototype. As she watched, the four jets rotated, in perfect synch, into horizontal position and the craft took off, circling the plateau and performing a loop and roll in a display of aerobatics. When it circled back and hovered again twenty yards away from Artemis, a double-barreled shotgun was protruding from the cockpit. The pilot fired a shot into the rock wall above her head. Then he leaned out, shouting into a bullhorn over the quietly humming jets.

"That's a warning, Fletcher! Turn back and wait for me at base camp. Duncan Sinclair has some business to settle with you. Vacate this area at once!"

Artemis was already cocking her crossbow. She fired directly into the air intake of one of the jet engines. Her bolt jammed the fan blades, sending mangled shards whirling into the compressor. As metal parts and afterburner fuel began spewing out of the exhaust, Artemis was already nocking her second bolt. Feeling a twinge of remorse at bringing down such a fascinating machine, she pulled the trigger. Her aim, at a second engine, was dead accurate. With two engines out, the craft was no longer able to hover or move forward. It dropped straight down and landed hard on the plateau. Tom Doyle crawled out, bruised, scraped, and dazed. He dropped his pack on the ice and cocked the shotgun. Unsteady on his feet, he was slow bringing the gunstock to his shoulder.

Artemis had time to push Norbu to the ice and lay flat on top of her just as Doyle got off a double-barreled shot. The report echoed off the ice cliffs, repeating and blooming until it turned into a sound like thunder. The mountainside began to shake, and the thunder was magnified a hundredfold. Artemis and Norbu made it to the cave where the Sherpas were hiding just as the snow field on the peak above them began to move. The avalanche carried the lightweight aircraft like a toy, along with Doyle's backpack and shotgun. The gear was swallowed by a crevasse that might have been thousands of feet deep. Doyle was clinging to a boulder that followed the slide downhill, vanishing into a cloud of frost thrown up by the tumult. In five minutes, all was silent again except for the wind.

Artemis and Norbu were unharmed except for a few scratches and bruises. They turned on their headlamps and ventured deeper into the cave. The passage narrowed until it looked impossible to go further, but beyond, they could hear chanting.

"Om mani padme hum."

They followed the sound through a narrow opening into a gallery, where their headlamps revealed the three Sherpas lying prostrate on the cave floor, repeating the mantra. They were facing two oak chests, with the lids thrown open. Extending from them were the still-shiny cylinders containing the *thangka* paintings. The two women waited respectfully while the Sherpas made their observance. It was getting late in the afternoon. The five of them worked together to lash the trunks securely onto the ever patient yaks. They started down the mountain.

Babu led the way, followed by his two fellow Sherpas, who kept an eye on the cargo as the pack animals carried it across the deck of the rope bridge. Norbu followed, giving Artemis a chance to observe the gliding walk once more. As she reached the halfway point, the mountain seemed to groan as a rock outcropping holding the south main cable cracked. Norbu broke her gliding stride and ran to safety on the downhill ledge just as the cable came loose and the weight of the deck planks broke the second cable. The bridge tumbled into the crevasse, leaving four climbers and two yaks on the downhill side, and Artemis alone on the uphill side. She shouted across.

"I have my sleeping bag and Hershey bars in my pack. I even have coffee, matches, and kerosene. I'll be fine until morning."

Norbu pointed west, where the sun was sinking.

"There is another rope bridge a quarter mile that way. It was replaced last spring. Should be safe. Wait until daylight so you don't lose your way up here, Artemis. I know it looks deserted, but there are wolves, tigers, and snow leopards in these mountains!"

"Don't worry, Norbu. I'm like Paladin. Have crossbow, will travel!"

CHAPTER 37

ILL MET BY MOONLIGHT

Artemis unrolled her down-filled bag and slept until she smelled the coffee. That would normally be a good thing, but not when one is supposedly alone on a remote mountain. She opened her eyes. It was still dark. The red-haired man was standing over her can of kerosene, warming his hands. She tried to move her own hands. They were tied.

"I don't believe we've been properly introduced, ma'am. I'm Tom Doyle. I know who you are. Looks like you would have owed old Duncan Sinclair a hefty bill for that prototype up there, Fletcher. That is, if you had made it down the mountain alive."

"I'm alive right now. If you had the guts to kill me, why didn't you do it last night while I was asleep? The crevasse is right there. No evidence."

"Fletcher, Fletcher, where is your imagination? I could toss you over the edge and hike down the mountain, but what kind of story would that make back at the club? No, you're a legend, you need a legendary end to your saga. You're interested in Buddhism, right? Have you ever heard of sky burial? That's when the deceased is left on top of a mountain for the vultures. It's considered quite an honor by the monks. Return to nature and all of that. Wouldn't it be interesting to experience it while you're still alive? As you mentioned, no evidence. The vultures would take care of that."

He took a sip from the coffee cup, then casually kicked her crossbow across the rocks. It disappeared into the crevasse, falling so far that the clattering simply faded out.

"It sure was awful kind of you to include coffee in your pack for our little camping trip. Can't start the day without coffee. Too bad my backpack went down yesterday, what with your letter and all in it."

He drained the tin cup.

"Well, time's a wastin'."

He pulled a .38 revolver out of his jacket.

"Let's get hiking. It's almost daylight."

They trekked up toward the plateau. Going was slow, across fields of loose rock. They kept their heads down and stepped gingerly. Artemis thought about making a break, but to where? Plunging off the trail in this terrain would be riskier than dealing with Doyle.

When they reached the high rock field where he crashed the day before, Doyle tightened Artemis's wrist bonds, tied her ankles together, and carried her to a flat boulder, open to the sky.

"We had a little saying in the Navy. When the ship was sinking and the water was up to your neck, you'd say, 'Another fine day.' Well, it looks like this is another fine day for you, Miss Fletcher. I'd love to hang around and do a little bird watching, but I've got to get down this mountain and fetch those paintings."

He turned and headed down the rock trail.

CHAPTER 38

THE TURQUOISE GODDESS

The vultures began circling within a few minutes. They were in no hurry. Artemis worked the rope around her wrists, but Doyle's knots were Navy knots, not Boy Scout knots. They held. As the sun reached midday, it was hard for her eyes to follow the birds as they circled lower and lower. She felt hypoxia coming on. She was growing sleepy and too weak to chafe any longer against her bonds. As she drifted off to sleep, she whispered one word.

"Hamsa."

When she woke, the sun's glare had moved west. She blinked and realized that the vultures were gone. One massive bird was circling overhead. It circled downward and perched next to her. It was the goose from the temple in Katmandu. The bird spoke to Artemis.

"I am Hamsa, the mother. I am also Palden Lhamo, the turquoise goddess. I guard this peak. You know me as Sky Woman. I know who you are as well. You are Artemis the wild huntress. You will not die today, Artemis. Your hunt is eternal. My grandson Wulver saw that in you at the dam, when you might have died then and there. I saw it in you when you came to my palace, when I was the Kumari."

Her beak easily snapped the ropes on Artemis's wrists and ankles.

"Now I must get you down from Cho Oyu before dark. Close your eyes and go back to sleep, Artemis."

Hamsa chanted in Sanskrit over her langorous charge, and the sleeping woman dissolved into a rainbow constellation of light waves that reassembled into a downy chick. The mother goose cradled the gosling in her feathers as she flew down thousands of feet to the boulders just above base camp. The Sherpas who saw the great bird land were not surprised when a dazed Artemis emerged from the rocks unharmed, rubbing her eyes. They understood.

Twenty-four hours later she was in the hot tub at Dwarika's Hotel. The attendant made casual conversation.

"How was your trip to our beautiful mountains, madam?"

"Lovely, but of course I was combining pleasure with business."

"And all with a lovely outcome, one hopes?"

"It was a fine day, *sathi*. A fine day."

CHAPTER 39

DOYLE'S DILEMMA

Tom Doyle spent the next night after coming down off the mountain in the hotel bar at Dwarika's. He met up with a pair of Navy ensigns on leave, and the American beer flowed as he regaled them with stories about his brave exploits, including single-handedly resolving the Cuban missile crisis the previous fall.

"You were UDT, a real frogman?"

"That's right lads, the boldest of the bold. Underwater demolition was my stock-in-trade. If you ever need a sub blown up, give me a call!"

The three men laughed raucously, and while they were toasting all around at the bar, Artemis Fletcher walked to the front desk across the lobby, checked her messages, and carried her suitcase to a waiting taxi.

In the morning, Doyle walked to the Western Union office and wired Iverson.

GOOD NEWS. TARGET ELIMINATED. SLIGHT PROBLEM
WITH AIRCRAFT. WILL UPDATE ON THANGKA
PROGRESS. DOYLE.

Doyle gulped coffee and aspirin while he waited for Iverson's response. After twenty minutes, the Western Union agent called out from his desk.

"Response to your wire, sir."

Doyle read Iverson's response.

CORRECTION. PAINTINGS ARRIVED DHARAMSHALA
YESTERDAY. DALAI LAMA PROBABLY ADMIRING
THIS VERY MOMENT. ONE MORE CHANCE BEFORE
I GO TO SINCLAIR. MOVE TO THE YMCA.
AWAIT FURTHER ORDERS.

Doyle scratched his head. He had a feeling his honeymoon with the Strabo Society might be over.

PART THREE

The Shogun View

CHAPTER 40

THE FABLE AND FAIRY TALE CLUB

Alexander Wolfe looked forward to the monthly meetings of the Fable and Fairy Tale Club. He started the club because he thought it would be something entirely fitting for the library serving Washington Irving's home turf. It proved to be popular with the townsfolk, and the members would all read the same spooky story before each meeting came around, always on the dark of the moon.

The club members savored the local touchstones in the legends of Sleepy Hollow and Rip Van Winkle. Most of the club members were retired adults who, as kids, had thrilled to Boris Karloff as Frankenstein's monster and Lon Chaney as the Wolf Man.

The latter had a special resonance for the locals, given the chaotic events out in Scarborough just three years earlier. At the end of November the subject came up.

"Mr. Wolfe, what's your opinion about that creature, the creature north of town?"

He closed his book and smiled.

"The Lenape people who called this area home for ten thousand years had a sacred symbol, the enchanted wolf, so to them a man or woman who could turn into a creature would be someone very special, not a monster. Perhaps that would symbolize for them that humans are part of nature, not separate from it, and shape shifting would be a gesture of unity with the planet."

"But the terror. The whole town was up in arms! What do you think, was there really a monster living in that old gatehouse?"

"Well, having read most of the books in this building…"

Wulver looked around at the stacks.

"I tend to think that anything is possible."

He glanced at his watch.

"Eight o'clock! No meeting in December. In January we'll discuss an old Italian folk tale, the lycanthrope of Ravello. Have a great holiday, everyone!"

When the last guest had departed, Wulver locked the front and side doors of the library and brewed himself a cup of tea. He loved being alone in the silent building after hours, surrounded by his beloved books. The dark of the moon was a time of rest and meditation for him, when the stirrings were stilled.

He flipped through a stack of unopened letters on his desk. One bore the return address:

A. Fletcher
Sakara Hotel
Kyoto, Japan

He opened it.

Dear Alistair,

So much to tell you. I encountered Sky Woman on two occasions recently. She saved my life in the Himalayas. I find myself feeling more and more that Sky Woman is protecting me, wherever the Agency sends me around the globe. I know you could help me understand why a goddess has adopted me!

I am in Kyoto practicing sword combat. My crossbow vanished down a Himalayan crevasse. I'll build a new one, someday when I get home to Valhalla.

Stay safe, my friend.

Artemis

CHAPTER 41

BALANCE

It was not Artemis Fletcher's first trip to Kyoto. When she was twenty, she was the first Westerner ever invited to compete in the ancient samurai archery tournament, held every January at the Sanjūsangen-dō Temple. The tournament was not on the temple grounds, but actually inside the temple. The twelfth-century building was the longest wooden structure in Japan, and it was possible to set the small target a full sixty yards from the archers. For eight centuries, kimono-clad young women competed as a rite of passage to adulthood. There were still many in Kyoto who recalled the astonishing young American who displayed not only skill, but a samurai-like focus and calm as she "became the arrow" and scored her bullseye to win.

With her sabbatical still in effect until the spring semester, Artemis decided to take some time for herself. She was, for the moment, a crossbow expert without a weapon, her piece having vanished down a Himalayan crevasse. Looking to broaden her horizons, she booked a flight to Japan, intending to revisit the site of her youthful archery triumph, enjoy a bit of the freedom of anonymity, and hopefully delve deep into the study of traditional swordsmanship. At home she was a teacher; abroad she was a perpetual student. She secured a flight direct from India to the ancient Buddhist holy city, Kyoto.

Before her flight out of New Delhi, Artemis made one last trip to the Daryaganj Book Mart, to thank Birindar and pick up a copy of Musashi's *Book of Five Rings*. On the flight to Japan, she read the seventeenth-century samurai swordsman's entry titled "Water." The instructions were not on sword-wielding, but on maintaining balance. She was well aware that her mistake on the Kensico Dam—the mistake that would have cost her life if the wolverine had not been capable of compassion—was a miscalculation of balance; her stance was unsteady. With her latest crossbow now buried deep in the ice of the Himalayas, she was going to Kyoto to enter a dojo, where she could perfect her skill with the *kitana*, the sword that Musashi used in his undefeated career.

Artemis established her base at the Sakara Hotel, in the Higashiyama District. The leafy narrow streets, the old two-story wooden buildings, and the ever present forest and Eastern Mountains reminded her of hamlets in the Hudson Valley. She could stroll from the hotel a few blocks north to the great gate of the Yasaka Shrine.

At the great gate, she felt the heart of the old city beating. She went there when she felt the isolation of her studies and the weight of the secrets that she held inside. The sincerity of the pilgrims centered her. From Yasaka, it was just a few blocks into the Gion District, the neighborhood of the *geiko*, or the geisha, as the tourists called them. They lived in *okiya*, communal houses, in the employ of an *oka-san*, an older woman who served not only as their boss but foster mother as well. The *oka-san* was not a "madam," and the *geiko* were not prostitutes. They entertained with music and traditional dance in the *ochaya*, or teahouses. The experienced *geiko* acted as *onee-san*, older sisters, training the apprentice *maiko*. Gion was a world of women and women-owned business. Artemis loved to stroll the quiet Shirakawa precinct of the neighborhood, along the Biwa canal, bowing respectfully to the *geiko* in their elaborate kimono and makeup as they made their way to work.

CHAPTER 42

THE HIKE

Artemis returned from her *katana* sword class and stopped at the front desk to check for messages. The clerk pointed in the direction of the outdoor courtyard.

"You have a guest, Miss Fletcher."

A young man rose and bowed as she entered the courtyard. He wore Levi's and a New York Yankees jersey.

"Miss Fletcher, my name is Aki. I am a friend of Mr. Langley."

Artemis smiled and nodded, sensing that the tranquility of her sojourn in Kyoto was coming to an end.

Aki said, "I would like to suggest an afternoon hike. There are some lovely views from the Eastern Mountains."

"Give me twenty minutes to get ready."

Aki bowed. "Of course."

As they walked, Aki explained that he was born in Kyoto but graduated from Princeton with a degree in international affairs, then took his advanced studies at Kyoto University, with a specialty in East Asian art history. He didn't elaborate on his connection with the Agency, nor did Artemis expect him to.

They chatted as they walked up the Keage Incline, a long former railbed lined with cherry trees that would blossom in April. They turned left at a red gate and started up the Isshu Trail toward the Shōgunzuka Viewpoint. At the top, most hikers entered the historic temple. Aki suggested that they head straight to the viewpoint looking south over Kyoto, all the way to Osaka. They were alone there.

"We can talk now. Miss Fletcher, have you visited the San-jūsangen-dō Temple?"

"I fired an arrow inside that temple."

Aki raised an eyebrow. He was too young to recall firsthand the American girl who once earned her samurai status in the great hall, but he had heard the story from his mother and aunts.

"So that was you. Well, you may need to fire another arrow in there if things continue to play out the way they are at the moment."

Artemis was fully focused, waiting for her instructions.

"Having been there, you have seen the massive statue of Kannon, the goddess of mercy, and if you have seen that, you have surely seen the five hundred smaller statues of Kannon to her left, and the five hundred to her right. Each one was hand carved from cypress and covered in gold eight centuries ago, and each one has an individual face, just like we do."

"I remember. There are a thousand and one goddesses in that hall, and still space for an archery contest."

"Correct. Now, let me show you something."

He pulled a manila folder from his backpack.

"The agency intercepted a pouch sent to the YMCA in Kathmandu last week. We have had a contact in the mailroom there since the special operation in 1959. He recognized that the diplomatic insignia was fake. Miss Fletcher, are you familiar with the Strabo Society?"

"They tried to kill me on a mountaintop in Nepal last week, so I would say yes."

"That would be Doyle. Red hair?"

"He introduced himself by firing a shotgun at me from a helicopter. A little while later he tried to finish the job by tying me down on a mountain as a dinner entree for a flock of vultures."

"But you're here, aren't you?"

"You know the job description, Aki."

"Doyle wired the Society with the news that you were confirmed dead. That's why you were chosen for this mission. It's fortunate that you are already in Kyoto. You're the last person he would expect to encounter."

"By that you mean Doyle is in Kyoto now?"

"He checked in to the Sakanoue last week. He's been carousing in the Gion every night with a trio of known *yakuza*."

"Mobsters."

"Correct. They have been on our radar for a long time. They're linked to every major art heist in the past decade, but no government has been able to pin anything solid on them. We're making an educated guess that Doyle will be their undoing. He likes to party. The Agency had two men disguised as Navy ensigns tail him around the expat bars in Kathmandu. A few beers and he would start bragging about his upcoming job in Japan. That's when this came into our hands."

He glanced left and right, then removed a paper from the folder and handed it to her. It was a letter, typed on Strabo Society letterhead.

Doyle,

Sinclair is not happy with the botched thangka job, nor is he

*happy about the prototype. He called in favors from here all
the way to RAF headquarters in High Wycombe to make that
thing available. You were warned that Fletcher was armed and
dangerous. It was naive of you to think she couldn't bring down
an aircraft with just a crossbow. If she's out of the picture, so much
the better for you. You were punching above your weight class, and
I don't mind telling you so.*

*When you arrive in Kyoto, check in at the Sakanoue. The desk clerk
will have the address of a teahouse where you will rendezvous at
8 PM with our three associates in Japan. Finalize the plan for
acquisition of statue A3 with them.*

*Doyle, you are on thin ice with Sinclair. He's not a man you want
to cross. He has global reach. Enough said. Don't screw this up.
Iverson.*

Aki returned the folder to his backpack, and they hiked back down the mountain. At the base of the Keage Incline, he handed her a business card.

"Go to this address this evening at 5 p.m. Ask for the proprietress. Her name is Amaya. Tell her you are inquiring about *henshin*. She is a friend of Mr. Langley. Follow her instructions from that point."

Aki bowed, wished Artemis the best of luck, and ducked into the metro station, leaving her to stroll the leafy streets back to the hotel. She would need to dress in a neutral, natural way to meet her new *oka-san*.

CHAPTER 43

THE FLOWER AND WILLOW WORLD

The *okiya* was a narrow row house Artemis had passed frequently on her canal-side walks through Shirakawa. Because it housed the *geiko* during the day, when they were out of character, there was no indication that it was anything other than a small apartment house.

A young *maiko*, not yet made up for the evening, answered the door and escorted Artemis inside. The narrow façade concealed the actual layout of the place. The building extended far back from the street, with stairways leading up to the dormitories, and studios on the ground floor where *henshin*, the transformation, took place. Artemis was surprised that Amaya, the house mother, dispensed with the traditional formal bow and embraced her, European style. She spoke with a French accent.

"Miss Fletcher, welcome to the flower and willow world. Aki has prepared us for your arrival. May I call you Artemis? It's a beautiful name. The wild huntress. I understand that you will be hunting, perhaps hunting the one who has hunted you, but we will say no more about that. It is time for your *henshin*, your transformation into a *maiko,* an apprentice. Tonight you will train with your new older sister, your *onee-san.* Her name is Kyoko. Your name tonight is Hatsuko, the child. Now, I must return to my work. Kyoko will guide you for the remainder of the evening. *Ganbatte,* Hatsuko, good luck."

Kyoko guided Artemis from studio to studio, where she was fitted for her kimono with white brocade collar, *obi* waistband and belt, and *okobo* platform shoes with button socks. Her blond locks disappeared under a jet-black wig. Then she was made up with *oshiroi,* ivory white makeup, with red eye shadow and fine black outlines around her eyes, eyebrows, and lips. When she was shown the mirror, she felt that she was looking at a work of traditional Japanese art, and it filled her with humility and respect. Looking at her image in the mirror, she thought, *This is powerful. This is art. This is womanhood, and this is to be respected.*

Kyoko, her older sister for the evening, was a graduate of the London School of Dramatic Arts. In perfect English, she filled her apprentice in on the evening's mission as they walked to the tea house.

"The men you are surveilling meet at the same *ochaya* every evening around half past eight. They ignore the *geiko* except to make the odd crude comment. They rent a private room and drink *sake* until ten. We will be wallpaper to them, which is ideal. I will begin playing the *taiko* drum. Follow my rhythm. I will do a traditional dance while you continue to drum softly. The room is small. Listen closely to the men. The American does not understand Japanese, so the other three will speak in English, except when they ridicule him among themselves. If they address you, smile and bow politely. Show no understanding at all of English. Here we are. Ready, Hatsuko?"

CHAPTER 44

THE MAIKO

The four men were seated on pillows around a low table in the private room. They were toasting with small clay tumblers of *sake* when the two women entered. The men ignored them as they arranged themselves in traditional posture and began to softly beat their *taiko* drums. Kyoko nodded, smiling in a ritual pose to her little sister as she put down the drum and began to dance. The steps were formal, theatrical, nothing like the kind of dancing that American men might consider entertaining at a stag party. One of them, the tall one with red hair, was downing cups of *sake* and laughing loudly at his own jokes. The others rolled their eyes and commented in Japanese. Kyoko suppressed a smile and continued dancing. The men were drunken louts, but they were also dangerous criminals. The two women knew they were no safer than if they had entered a cage of tigers. The red-haired man slammed his *choko-o* cup down on the table and spoke, slurring his words, to his co-conspirators.

"These dames have no idea what we're saying. Let's lay this

plan out once and for all. I know the statue is in a temple. How do we get it out?"

"It is not the only statue in the temple. In fact there are a thousand and one statues in the temple."

"What the...?"

"We have a diagram of the exact location of the specific piece your boss desires. That will not present a problem. We will arrive at midnight tomorrow in a *reikyusha*, traditional Japanese hearse. The casket will contain the tools we need to dislodge the statue, which will then be placed in the casket. As we depart the temple grounds, anyone spotting us will bow and say a silent prayer for the deceased. You will arrive on foot and disable the monk who guards the service entrance. Mr. Doyle, your reputation for excess precedes you. I must advise you not to injure a Buddhist monk. You are a guest in our country."

"Sure, whatever. I can tie him up and gag him. He'll be as good as new in the morning, guarding his exactly one thousand statues."

"So we meet at midnight tomorrow at the service entrance, Sanjūsangen-dō Temple."

The men exited without a glance at the two women.

CHAPTER 45

THE BOW

Artemis visited the great hall in the early afternoon. Photography was forbidden inside, but she had an indelible memory of her first visit, years earlier. The massive interior space was crowded with noisy spectators back then. On this particular day, though, the only crowd was a silent one; five hundred gold statues stood to the right of the central figure, and another five hundred to the left. She bowed respectfully and stood, eyes downward, before the mother of compassion, Kannon. Artemis whispered to the bodhisattva.

"I know you are the great mother, the avatar of Avalokiteśvara, the Blessed Virgin, Isis, Gaia. I know you as the little Kumari in her palace, as the mother goose who cut my bonds, and I know you as Sky Woman in the high peaks. You have protected me. Tonight I am tasked with protecting you. Grant me peace, tranquility, and balance when I return here."

Her prayer complete, Artemis took a moment to locate statue A3, based on the chart the Agency intercepted. She returned to the Sakara. The desk clerk hailed her.

"Your friend Aki left a large object for you. The bellman delivered it to your room."

Artemis's forehead crinkled as she unlocked her door and entered slowly. On the day of a mission, it was wise to err on the side of caution. Leaning against her desk was a six-foot *kyudo* bow, the kind used by Zen masters, the kind she had used to win the tournament years before. A quiver of arrows was laid on the bed. Artemis sat *zazen*, meditating on *om*, centering. At 11:15 she put in a call to Kyoto Prefectural Police Headquarters. Then she laced her Doc Martens and headed for the temple.

CHAPTER 46

THE THOUSAND AND ONE
GODDESSES

Artemis was crouched beneath a cherry tree when the hearse turned onto the park-like grounds surrounding the temple. As the vehicle pulled out of sight behind the north side of the long building, she sprinted around the south side to a utility door. During the afternoon, she had made a clay cast of the keyhole. She already knew which one of her ring of skeleton keys would fit. Once inside, she made her way to statue B3, directly across from the thieves' target.

An hour seemed to pass in the darkness, although it was actually only five minutes before the side door opposite her hiding place opened. Four men in hooded sweatshirts entered, carrying the casket like pallbearers. They laid it next to the back row of statues on their side of the temple and opened the lid. Artemis wanted to stop them, but if she made her presence known before the police had the temple surrounded, the *yakuza* would likely escape, vanishing into the Gion. Doyle was her target. She had no intention of letting him walk out of that temple without handcuffs on.

The tall man had jammed a crowbar under the gold statue and was putting the weight of his right leg on it when the rotating lights of police cars illuminated the side door. The three thugs made a dash for the opposite door, the one Artemis had entered. She stood up, turned on her headlamp, and shouted, "Police, *teishi!*"

She flashed the light from one man to another, shining directly in their eyes. In the glare, they were lost in the maze of statues, bumping from one to the next and into each other. The police had both side doors covered when Artemis shouted across the hall at Doyle.

"Police. Hands up!"

He dropped the crowbar, pulled his .38 out of his sweatshirt pouch, and fired one wild shot before turning to run toward the massive front doors. Artemis had checked the main entrance during the afternoon. Locked, it couldn't be opened from the outside, but from the inside, fire regulations required it to be opened by pressing on a brass crossbar.

There was no way she could catch up to him running down the concourse of the huge hall. She picked up the samurai bow and felt the string for a nock point. She found it. She pulled an arrow from the quiver and nocked it. This would be her first time using this bow, the first time feeling the string tension, but there was no time to think about that. She could only see as far as her headlamp, and Doyle was disappearing out of its beam of light. Artemis glanced up at the central statue of Kannon. She felt the dream again, the dream from Kumari's palace in Nepal. Time stood still while the goddess's face softened. She whispered to Artemis.

"Artemis, you are the wild huntress, the daughter of the moon. My own daughter. Remember your balance and become like water."

Artemis turned. It was a good sixty yards to Doyle. The same sixty yards she had shot as a twenty-year-old, in the same great hall. She aimed and released the bowstring.

The arrow caught her target, the crown of Doyle's hood, as he reached the massive oak doors. He made the panicked mistake of trying to dislodge the arrow from the wood before realizing it would be easier to wriggle out of the sweatshirt. By then it was too late. Artemis looped twine around his wrists as they came free of the sleeves and tied a lightning-fast constrictor knot. She ducked as he swung his bound arms at her, pulled his legs out from under him at the knees, and tied his ankles in a bowline knot.

She flipped him over so he could see her face. His eyes widened in disbelief.

"Fletcher?"

"Sorry, Doyle. Looks like it's another fine day for you."

She left him hog-tied as the police approached, bowing in thanks. She smiled, bowing, and then walked alone to the central statue of Kannon. She laid the bow and quiver of arrows at the gold statue's feet, bowed, whispered *"Arigato,"* and walked out into the moonlit cherry garden.

CHAPTER 47

HOME

December brought changes to the Strabo Society. Duncan Sinclair, age eighty-three, passed away at Southampton Hospital, of liver failure.

An anonymous tip to the FBI's Manhattan office led to a raid on the Strabo clubhouse. Charles Iverson shredded his "eyes only" file before he gave up the combination to the third-floor vault in exchange for a reduced sentence in Danbury Federal Prison on multiple charges of conspiracy to commit international art theft.

Tom Doyle was charged with desecration of a sacred site and sentenced to twenty years in Yamashina Prison.

The day after Christmas, Alex Wolfe looked up from his desk at the sound of a familiar voice.

"Excuse me, sir, is there an opening in the Fable and Fairy Tale Club?"

"Artem—"

She raised a finger to her lips and whispered.

"Merry Christmas, Alistair."

CHAPTER 48

THE DECISION

January 1964, Westchester County

Artemis Fletcher spent the two weeks before the Sarah Lawrence spring semester assembling the notes from her exploration of the alleyways in Lyon. She was also busy writing a proposal to include East Asia in her medieval history curriculum. There were book outlines, class schedules, and lesson plans to write. Her desk was in a glass-walled office at the rear of her sprawling home on the Atalanta estate. She could look out on the swimming pool, her crossbow target range, and a cedar-shingle cabin that her father had built. That cozy shed was her lair and hideout when she was a teen, but it had remained vacant in the years since she grew into her dual career as educator and adventurer.

On a snowy January day, Artemis and Wulver stood looking out over the Kensico Reservoir.

"Alex, you have come so far. You have a social life at the library. When spring comes, you'll be taking the Tadpole Club on field trips all over the county. No one knows the trails and rivers around here better than you. You are passing your love of nature and books on to a generation. You have reason to be proud."

Wulver was silent for a while, looking out at the pond.

"I am tired, Artemis. The stirrings…They only subside on the dark of the moon. You can't know what it means to pass beyond mortality, but still be marooned here. What you see as my love of nature is my desire to fully return to it. The separation that I feel… It's the Buddha's radical statement that all of life is suffering. Only the immortal understand what he meant. We long to return."

"Alex, I want you to move into the cottage. You can walk over the hills before dawn every morning to the library, and in the evenings we can work through these things together."

She paused.

"And Cranberry Lake is just down the trail, when you need to make your way to the quarry. You will be safer here in Valhalla."

"Artemis, I was accosted as I left the library one evening last week by a man, a private detective. He addressed me as Alistair Wulver, not Alexander Wolfe. He was working for a law firm in the city. I don't know how he found me. It seems that Lethe Van Leer's will was found in the Strabo Society vault. The lawyers followed a paper trail and located his death certificate at the city hall in Venice, Italy. They also learned that the Scarborough property never passed from his hands. He left it to me."

Artemis caught her breath.

"You're a rich man, Alex. That's millionaire's row."

"I've already retained a real estate agent to sell it. Half of the money will go to the library. With the other half I want to establish a scholarship fund in Van Leer's name. It will pay for young women to learn your kind of syncretic knowledge: history, world literature, Eastern wisdom, martial arts, mythology. I want you to run the program."

"You don't want to keep the money, maintain a wealthy life-style? The men who hunted us are gone, Alex. You can rejoin society."

"I want to rejoin the earth, Artemis."

They walked down the long stairs and took the path toward the back gate of Atalanta. He paused at the door of the cabin.

"I look forward to wintering here at the cottage. In the spring I will show the Tadpole Club the places where I learned to love nature as a boy, and I will steer them to the books that inspired me. With the donations in place, I will have done my work. Then I will go to the Church of the Magdalene up in Pocantico Hills and make my confession. I am ready."

CHAPTER 49

THE PASSAGE

By mid-April, the ice was gone from Floodwood Pond. Snow still lay in scattered drifts, and icy cascades clung to the rocks in shady spots as Artemis's Jeep, pulling two canoes on a trailer, made its way into the heart of the Adirondacks. The dirt road into the Saint Regis Wilderness was muddy but passable. The truck bounced over the ruts and came to a stop at the remains of the old Dubois cabin, where Wulver had wintered alone for forty years. She hauled the canoes down to the shore, letting him stand alone on the porch, looking out over the water. She could hear him chanting softly. After ten minutes, he walked straight to the put-in. They paddled in separate canoes to the southern end of the lake and pulled alongside at the nameless island where Wulver had undergone his transformation so long ago. Herons and mergansers fished in the shallows, as the cool evening breeze of early spring wafted through the boughs of big white pines.

As the shadows grew long, the first loon of the evening called, and its mate across the lake answered. More loons joined in the otherworldly chorus. A horned owl beat its wings overhead, and then a golden eagle, looping slowly, descended from her pride of place. Artemis collected tinder, kindling, and birch logs for a fire. When the flames leapt and the logs crackled, Wulver lay peacefully in the radiant aura. The horned owl and the golden eagle perched on a downed oak. The four of them remained silent for a long time. Then Deganawida, in his warrior body, began to chant quietly, a song of release. He rubbed oil on Wulver's forehead and prayed over him. Wulver's breathing slowed. Deganawida lifted him and carried him to his canoe. He laid his son on the keel with his head at the bow and placed a burning birch limb in the stern. He pushed the canoe off, letting it drift freely with only Wulver's sleeping form aboard.

Artemis, Deganawida, and Sky Woman watched as the canoe drifted out to the center of Floodwood Pond. The flames enveloped the elmwood, and then suddenly vanished as the canoe went down. The two great birds took flight across the lake. Artemis extinguished the birch fire and set out toward the cabin. As she paddled, the loon's wild cries rose to a crescendo, then the tumult subsided as darkness fell. Artemis smiled and thought of a line from Tennyson:

"Long stood Sir Bedivere / Revolving many memories, till the hull / Look'd one black dot against the verge of dawn, / and on the mere the wailing died away."

EPILOGUE

October is the month of leafy splendor in Westchester County, and the month of spooky lore, in the tradition of author and local resident Washington Irving. Every village along Route 9 is decked out in ghostly decorations, and the hamlet of Sleepy Hollow hosts a parade led by the headless horseman of legend. A bit north in Scarborough, the village sponsors a haunted hayride that skirts the old Sparta Cemetery and dips down the weed-choked road into the long-abandoned Acheron estate. Last year, a few hayride patrons complained of a musky smell hanging in the air in the vicinity of the crumbling ruins of the gatehouse. A vagrant skunk, no doubt…

www.ingramcontent.com/pod-product-compliance
Lightning Source LLC
Chambersburg PA
CBHW051139020726
47501CB00005B/1582